Nutty
Knows
All

BOOKS BY DEAN HUGHES

Nutty for President
Honestly, Myron
Switching Tracks
Millie Willenheimer and the Chestnut Corporation
Nutty and the Case of the Mastermind Thief
Nutty and the Case of the Ski-Slope Spy
Jelly's Circus
Nutty Can't Miss
Theo Zephyr
Nutty Knows All

Nutty Knows All

DEAN HUGHES

ATHENEUM 1988 NEW YORK

Atheneum
Macmillan Publishing Company
866 Third Avenue, New York, NY 10022
Collier Macmillan Canada, Inc.

First Edition
Printed in United States of America
10 9 8 7 6 5 4 3 2 1

Library of Congress Cataloging-in-Publication Data

Hughes, Dean,
Nutty knows all/by Dean Hughes.
p. cm.
Summary: Fifth-grader Nutty Nutsell produces another memorable
science fair project when his partner, William Bilks, transfers
photons of light to Nutty's brain, causing a personality change and
his head to glow in the dark.
ISBN 0-689-31410-8
[1. Science projects—Fiction. 2. Science—Experiments—Fiction.]
I. Title.
PZ7.H87312Nv 1988
[Fic]—dc19
88-886 CIP AC

Designed by Cathryn S. Aison

FOR JIM AND LINDA JACOBS

Nutty Knows All

"Nutty, what are you doing for your science project?" Orlando asked. "Do you think you can top last year's?" He put his arm around Nutty's shoulder and tried not to smile. But Bilbo and Richie both broke out laughing.

A couple of fifth-grade girls, who were also just coming out of class, heard Orlando and started laughing too. "He'd have to set off an atomic bomb to top last year's," one of them said.

Nutty pulled away from Orlando and kept walking. Some mistakes were funny after a while, but not the famous papier-mâché volcano. He knew he would be teased about the stupid thing for the rest of his life.

"It was a great volcano," Orlando said. "It just had lousy aim."

"Oh, I don't know. It hit everything in sight. That's pretty good shooting." Richie had a silly sort of laugh, kind of a giggle, and he wasn't even trying to hold it back.

Bilbo grinned his agreement, but then added, "Hey, don't knock it. It was the most exciting thing that happened all year—the only time that the whole Warrensburg fire department showed up at school."

"It was just two trucks," Nutty said, mostly to himself. The image all came back. The volcano was supposed to ooze lava, but as Nutty had dumped in the last of his chemicals, everything suddenly went crazy. The little mountain vibrated and started jumping around, and the papier-mâché sort of melted and caught fire, and then hot green stuff started shooting all over the place. Lava hit the ceiling and floor, and everything in between. In a couple of minutes the gym had filled with smoke and the chemical smell was spreading through the whole school.

"Did they ever make you pay for that table you ruined?" Richie asked. He and the other guys were walking fast now, trying to catch up with Nutty.

Nutty spun around, his blond hair flipping down over his forehead. He was taller than the other guys, but skinny, and when he put his hands on his hips to look mad, he looked like a stick man, not fearsome at all. "Lay off, you guys. I didn't ruin the table. It was just stained a little. They still use it."

"Yeah, down in the janitor's shop," Orlando said, his dark eyes full of mischief.

"Well—so what? Mr. Skinner needed a table down there."

"What else does he need, Nutty?" Richie said. "Maybe you can blow up something else for him this time around."

The guys liked that one. Bilbo leaned over on Richie and both of them laughed. Nutty couldn't help it. He started to smile too. "Well, maybe I've got something a lot better this year." He turned and walked quickly to his locker and went to work on his combination. He really wanted to get off this topic as fast he could.

But all three guys followed him. Orlando leaned against the locker next to Nutty's and said, "Oh, yeah? What is it?"

"Why should I tell you?"

"You haven't even started anything yet. You told me that on Friday," Orlando said.

"You don't know what I came up with over the weekend," Nutty responded as he fouled up the combination and had to start over.

"Nutty, you never did any school work over a weekend in your whole life, and you know it."

Nutty didn't respond to that one. The truth was, Orlando was right, but Nutty wasn't going to admit it. What he wanted to do—even decided to do—was to keep his mouth shut, but as usual the next thing he knew his mouth was moving before his brain had given it permission. "I'll tell you this much, guys. If you show up at the science fair with your little windmills and ant farms, you're going to be embarrassed. I'm not doing one of those 'I visited my uncle's farm and found out where milk comes from' kind of jobs. I've got something amazing this time."

"You don't either," Orlando said. "You're bluffing. There's no way you can come up with something that great in five days."

Five days? Was the science fair this Saturday? Somehow it hadn't hit Nutty that the thing was coming up quite that soon. "Orlando, has it ever occurred to you that I *wanted* you guys to think I didn't have anything? Did you ever stop to think that I might have been working on it for *weeks*?"

"No. It never occurred to me, and I never stopped to think of it. And not only that. I *know* you, and I know you haven't done a single thing."

Nutty was getting in deeper every second. He never knew why he did these things, but his lips were moving again, so he was sure he was about to make things worse. "Hey, this is all I'm saying for now. If I don't win the top award for the best project in the whole lab school, I'll be very surprised. It's going to take something *spectacular* to beat me out."

"Well, what are you going to do that's so hot?"

"I told you, I'm not saying anymore right now. You guys probably wouldn't understand it anyway. It's too scientific for you."

"Try me," Bilbo said. He had put his own hands on his hips. He was not quite as tall as Nutty, but he was stronger and, as Nutty also knew, he was smarter. He was always reading. In fact, he had gotten his nickname because he liked *The Hobbit* so much.

"Bilbo, I know you're pretty good in science, but I'm breaking new ground with my project. I'm—"

"Are you sure you're not breaking new table?" This was from Orlando, not Bilbo, but everyone laughed again.

"Okay, guys. Laugh all you want. Laugh until you cry. But when the fair is all over and I have that big purple ribbon, you guys will be the ones wishing you had thought up something as great as I did." Nutty stuck his books in his locker, pulled his blue Kansas City Royals jacket out, shut the door, and turned to walk away. But his first step took him into a head-on collision with Sarah Montag. He caught her in his arms, so she wouldn't fall backward, and for a moment, there they were, locked together like lovers on the cover of a romance novel.

Nutty jumped back. "Excuse me," he said.

Sarah's two friends started to giggle, but Sarah only smiled. "That's all right," she said.

Orlando let out with a long wooo-wooo. "Nutty, did you hear that? If it's all right, do it again."

"Shut up, Orlando." Nutty's face was now bright red. He liked Sarah, and everyone knew it. Besides that, Sarah liked him—and everyone knew that, too.

Richie said, "You'll have to excuse Nutty, Sarah. He's got his mind on some pretty heavy stuff, so it's hard for him to know where he's walking. He's thinking about his science project."

That's all it took. Sarah and the other girls immediately cracked up. "Not another volcano," one of them said.

"What is it this year, Nutty?" Sarah said. "An earthquake? Would you warn us this time before the building starts to shake apart?"

Nutty tried to smile. He could tell Orlando and the guys to jump in a lake, but he knew he had to show the girls he could take a little ribbing.

"Actually, I've got a very good project this year. I am sort of into science."

"Since when?"

All the girls were giggling, and Orlando was hooting, "Right, Nutty, right. You're always probing into the great mysteries of science."

"No, really. I like science." Nutty was speaking to Sarah, not to Orlando, and he was feeling like a bigger idiot every second. He could see that she wasn't taking him seriously. She had that flirty look on her face that she always used these days. Nutty liked her pretty smile, her dimples, even her funny laugh, but he didn't want her laughing at *him*.

"I think maybe you'd better stick with basketball, Nutty," Sarah said. "You get dangerous when you get chemicals in your hands." She reached up and patted him on the shoulder, even winked to show she was just teasing, but she walked away, and Nutty felt like a world-class jerk.

Nutty glanced at Orlando, who was sounding another one of his wooo-wooo's, and he decided to get out of there.

"You still haven't told us what your hot project is," Orlando yelled down the hallway after him.

Nutty didn't say a word. He had already said too much and he knew it. He was heading for the front doors.

"I know you don't have anything started, Nutty," Orlando yelled after him.

Nutty just kept walking.

"You'll start working on it Friday night."

No comment.

"And then your mother will end up doing most of it."

Nutty told himself not to answer, but his feet

quit walking and his mouth was suddenly off and running again. "You just keep thinking that, Orlando. But then I want to hear your apology when I show up with the best science project this school has ever seen."

Nutty went on out the door. He was mad. What did Orlando know? Why were the guys—and the girls—all so quick to assume the worst about him? They all seemed to think he couldn't do anything right—and they had no reason to judge him that way.

Of course, it *was* true that he had not started his project, had no idea what he was going to do, and had not even given it much thought. But they didn't know that; they were just jumping to conclusions.

Nutty continued to steam as he walked home. But as he was nearing his house his anger cooled a little and he started to admit something to himself: he was in trouble. "I've got to prove to those guys that I can do this," he muttered to himself. "I've got to show them I'm a lot smarter than they think. I've got to show them what I can do—on my own."

He let the implications of all that settle in for a time, and then he told himself, "I'd better go see William Bilks. I need help."

That afternoon when William Bilks got off his bus—
the one he took from the private school he at-
tended—Nutty was waiting for him at the bus stop.
"Nutty," he said, "what brings you here?"

"I've got a problem."

"Yes. I suppose I should have known that.
Walk home with me, and we'll see what we can do."

William looked the way he always did—like an
eleven-year-old escapee from a retirement home.
He had on his heavy coat, buttoned up to the throat,
his warm woolen scarf wrapped twice around his
neck, and furry little mittens. Spring was coming on
rather fast now, and most kids were wearing light

jackets. But then, William wasn't like most kids. Most kids weren't geniuses.

William may have looked like his usual self, but he didn't sound like himself. Nutty was picking up something strange in his manner. "Are you all right?" he asked.

"Yes. I suppose."

"You don't sound very happy."

"Oh, Nutty. Happy. What is happy? Most people live for such trivial purposes. For them a birthday party or some silly social event is reason enough for happiness. I require something more than that."

Nutty put his arm around little William's shoulder. "Gee, William, I know what you mean. I'm kind of depressed today too."

William glanced up, sort of rolled his eyes around, and then let his lungs empty out in a long, loud breath. Nutty wasn't sure what all that meant, but he decided to keep his mouth shut until they reached William's house. Nutty needed help, and he didn't dare get William in a bad mood.

When the boys reached William's bedroom, William removed his coat and hung it up in his closet; he folded his scarf and placed it neatly alongside his mittens in a drawer; he removed his shoes and slid on a comfy little pair of slippers; and then he walked around the room and gave a nod to each of the philosophers and scientists whose pictures were hanging on his walls. He greeted them all by name—from Plato and Aristotle down to Einstein. (William called him Albert.)

"Those are my friends," William said, and again his voice seemed unusually solemn. "They are the ones who understand me. I wish they could speak to me."

"Gee, William, you're really acting weird. Are you sure you're okay?"

"Yes, yes. Now—what is this great problem of yours? Did you quarrel with your little sweetheart?"

"Come on, William. I don't have a sweetheart, for crying out loud."

"Well, you have some sort of infatuation, as I recall. I believe you've fallen head over heels, as they say, for that little cheerleader with the dimples—Sarah something or other. Isn't that 'big stuff' with boys your age?"

"William, you're my age. You talk like you're an old man."

Actually Nutty knew that William always talked more or less that way, but he was pushing it today, going out of his way to remind Nutty of the gap between them. Nutty hardly needed any more of that sort of thing.

"Never mind me. What's the big problem?"

"Well, it's the science fair. I need to come up with something good this year."

William smiled for the first time, and then he chuckled in that grandfatherly way of his. He sat down on his desk chair, pushed up his glasses, and leaned back and folded his arms over his soft, round chest. "From what I heard, last year you gave your classmates something of a fright."

"Who told you that?"

"Orlando, I believe. Didn't you try to make a volcano erupt and end up—"

"Yeah, yeah. Never mind that. This year I've got to come up with something a lot better than that. Something really—you know—scientific."

"Well, yes. I think a science-fair project works out well if it's . . . scientific."

"I'm serious, William. I want to have something that will knock everyone's eyes right out."

"You came very near that last year."

"Lay off, okay? I've got to do something really intelligent. You know, brilliant . . . creative . . ."

"And that's why you want me to think it up."

"Well, not exactly." Nutty sat down on William's bed, leaned forward, and gave William his most serious look. "I don't want you to think it all up—or do it for me—or anything like that. I just need a hint, an idea, or something. I've been thinking and thinking and I can't come up with anything."

"My goodness, what a surprise! How long have you been working on it?"

"For more than an hour—ever since school got out today."

"Nutty, you thought for a whole hour? This is some sort of record."

Nutty stood up. "Okay, never mind," he said. "You think I'm a joke too—just like everyone at school. Well, I'm not as dumb as you think. I'm going to think up something on my own. It's going to be good too."

"Sit down, Nutty. Don't get so excited. And above all, don't try to do this thing on your own. You may end up taking human life. You got away lucky last time."

"That's not funny, William." Nutty grabbed his jacket and was about to leave.

"I'm sorry, Nutty," William said. "I really am. Please sit down. Let's see if we can't think of something. What sort of science concepts are you fellows working on in fifth grade these days?"

"Uh . . . I don't know. Let's see. We learned about the different kinds of clouds a while back."

"Couldn't you explain evaporation, and that sort of thing? You could set up one of those little cloud chambers. Isn't that what the children do at these—"

"William, what's with you? If I'm a child, so are you. Why are you talking this way today? You *do* think I'm dumb, don't you?"

"Not dumb, Nutty. You actually have more than your share of common sense, and you're a pretty good student, compared to other kids your age. But you mess up about three times a day, fumble your way along, and everyone sort of likes you because you don't threaten them. I suppose everyone feels that if *you* can survive this world, anyone can."

"William, I think that's a rotten thing to say. I don't mess up that much. And I'm a whole lot smarter than anyone knows. I'm going to go to the library right now and read up on some stuff. I'll see you." He stepped toward the door with an entirely new air of confidence. Unfortunately, however, he had hold of his jacket by only one sleeve. The other sleeve dragged on the floor, and Nutty somehow stepped on it. It tripped him up, and he went tumbling to his knees. He scurried up quickly, but his exit was ruined.

William started laughing—this time with some pleasure—and then, in spite of himself, Nutty laughed too. "Hey, that was just an accident," he said.

"It certainly was," William said, and his little round body bounced with pleasure.

"Look, William. I do want to get smarter. But you're going to have to help me, okay? Can't you think up something for me to do for the science fair—something that would shock the daylights out of the whole school?"

William motioned for Nutty to sit down. Nutty saw that wonderful distance come into William's eyes—that look he always got when he was delving into his bottomless pit of a mind, searching for an answer to one of Nutty's dilemmas.

But what William said, eventually, was anything but what Nutty expected. "Nutty, I've been working on a fascinating project, and I want to tell you about it."

"Sure, William, that's great. But about the science project. Couldn't you—"

"I'll get to that, Nutty. That's part of what I'm talking about. I've been working on some concepts lately that are both exciting and troubling. I want to explain them to you. I think we can create an experiment that you can use for a project. But I would like something more than that. I would like you to try to understand some difficult ideas, and I want you to probe some great questions with me."

"Okay," Nutty said. But for some reason, he felt a little frightened. William sounded so serious. "What kinds of things have you been working on? Is it chemistry or something, because I haven't had much of that sort of stuff yet."

"No. That's all right. It's all theoretical, and I can explain what you need to know. Just sit back and listen, and concentrate as hard as you can. Try to place yourself in the same state of deep concentration that I taught you when we were working on your basketball shooting. You'll need all your faculties."

Nutty thought a faculty was a bunch of teachers, but he didn't dare say that. He leaned back and tried to push his thoughts away, to clear his mind and be ready for some heavy stuff. What came to mind, however, was a hope that this wouldn't take too long because he was getting hungry.

"All right. First of all, you know about the atom—at least the basics. Nucleus, protons, electrons, that sort of thing."

"Yeah. Sort of."

William took a quick, disappointed look at Nutty. "Well, all right. Such particles are called sub-atomic—meaning smaller than the atom, or part of the atom. The study of sub-atomic particles is called quantum mechanics."

"What kind of mechanics?"

"Quantum. That refers to . . . well, never mind what that means, exactly. I'll give you some reading material. The point is that the entire world is made up of tiny particles that function in a kind of world of their own—inside the atom. We used to think that the atom was like a little solar system, but it turns out to be much more interesting than that. Particles within the atom don't work by the laws we are accustomed to. It's almost as though these particles have minds of their own."

"Wait a minute. Are you saying they have brains?"

"No. Not really. But then, we don't know. We

only know that they somehow seem to 'know,' in some sense of the word, what they are supposed to do."

"What *are* they supposed to do?"

"Good question. Let me give you an example. The tiny particles that make up light are called photons."

"Hey, wait." Nutty slid off the bed and onto the floor, so he would be closer to William, sitting at his feet, so to speak. "I think I've seen those. When the light is shining through the window, you can see little—"

"No, no, Nutty. Those are merely dust particles. And every particle of dust is made up of millions of atoms. There's no seeing a photon. It's much too small for that."

"Then what is light, anyway?"

"It's not easy to say what it is. But we know how it behaves—both as a wave, like a radio wave, and as a collection of particles, like electrons."

"I thought it floated around in the air."

William rolled his eyes again. "Nutty, just listen for a moment, okay?"

"Okay. Okay. Go ahead." Nutty crossed his arms and leaned back against the bed. He tried to look as serious as he could.

"In certain experiments, photons have behaved in ways that simply aren't explainable. When scientists shine light through two slits in a screen, the light that gets through and shines on the wall behind appears not as two stripes of light, as one would expect, but as a whole series of dark and light stripes. That's because the light is acting like waves. The photons are bumping into each other and forming a pattern—the same patterns waves always make. But here's the amazing part. If the scientist just shoots one photon at a time—so that there are no others to bump against—the individual photons still land where the stripes of light would be."

"Wait a minute. You lost me."

"The photons behave as though they are being bumped against, Nutty—even though they are all alone. It's like they know what would have happened, if all the photons had been moving at the same time, and so they do what they would normally do."

"But how? How could they know how to do that?"

"That's the problem. No one knows. But it would appear that photons—and maybe other sub-atomic particles—possess some sort of understanding. It's as though the photon has a certain kind of consciousness."

William paused dramatically. "Nutty, think of it. Perhaps there is some way to communicate with the particles that make up this world. Maybe they do have understanding. And maybe there's some way to get our understanding hooked up with theirs.

Suppose we could reach the consciousness of a photon. Who knows what might come of it? Maybe we could learn the inner secrets of the universe."

"Wow, this is hard," Nutty said. "Let me think for a minute." He got up and lay on the bed. He really wanted to understand what William was talking about—but he couldn't keep his mind off some more practical problems. "William," he finally said, "are you saying that my science project would be trying to talk to a bunch of little things that are floating around in light?"

"Yes, in a certain sense, that is what I'm saying. However, I would use the words 'communicate with,' not 'talk to.' I really don't know how we'll reach them—though I am working on some ideas. But it's exciting, isn't it, when you think of the possibilities?"

"Yeah, I guess. But what I'm wondering . . . if I sit there talking to a light bulb, or something like that, I think Orlando is going to make fun of me."

William had pushed his chair back again, but now he let the front legs crash back to the floor. At the same time William's arms flopped to his sides, and his head dropped back. He stared at the ceiling for a time, and then he finally said, "This isn't going to be easy."

Nutty had a feeling that maybe he had said the wrong thing.

3

When Nutty left William's house he was a little confused; by the time he got home he was nervous. William had tried to reassure him, had explained everything again, had even claimed that their work could be of major scientific importance. That was all well and good, but Nutty wasn't sure he could even explain the idea to anyone.

When Nutty got home he thought maybe he should do a little reading about atoms in the family's encyclopedia. But then he decided he needed a little rest and refreshment first. He dropped his jacket off in his bedroom, where it fell among a lot of other scattered and assorted debris, and he headed for the refrigerator.

"I'm getting dinner ready," his mother said. "You don't need to start eating everything in sight."

Nutty got himself a slice of bologna, wrapped it around a stalk of celery, and then slapped a thick layer of mustard all over it. He sat down at the kitchen table and took a big bite, which he washed down with a huge glass of grape juice.

"Oh, Freddie, that makes me sick," his mom told him.

Nutty was chewing. He took another big gulp of his drink and said, "Why, Mom? It's not even junk. It's all good, healthy stuff."

Nutty's little sister, Susie, came into the room and caught a view of Nutty's bologna-and-mustard treat. "Oh, *sick!*" she said. "Nutty, you've got half a bottle of mustard on that thing."

Nutty took a look. He did have plenty of mustard, but he liked the stuff. What was her problem? He shrugged, but didn't answer.

"Susie, don't call him Nutty. You know I hate that name."

"Why? That's what everyone calls him. If I called him Freddie at school, no one would know who I was talking about."

"I don't care. I don't like it. It makes him sound silly, or stupid, and he's not."

Susie flipped her pretty hair away from her eyes—her third-grade way of trying to seem glamorous—and said, "Well, a brain he's not."

"Come here a sec," Nutty said.

"Why?" Susie looked doubtful, but Nutty hadn't sounded angry. She walked over.

"Come closer. I want to tell you something." Nutty leaned forward to whisper in her ear.

She turned an ear toward him, and waited. Nutty said, softly, "If I'm so dumb, how did I just manage to paint your face with mustard?"

Susie jumped back, but it was too late. She had a yellow streak across her cheek. "Oh, gross. You're such a jerk, Nutty." She ran to the bathroom.

"For heaven's sake, Freddie," Mother said. "Why do you do things like that?"

"She said I was stupid. And she called me a jerk."

"She called you a jerk after you were one, and she didn't say you were stupid. She said you're not a brain. Are you?"

Nutty hoisted his legs up on the chair across from him and leaned back. "No, I'm not a brain. But it hurts my feelings when she talks to me that way. I'm a very sensitive boy."

He could see his mom trying not to smile, but she did anyway. "You're kind of nutty. That's what you are."

"Do you really think I'm not dumb, Mom?"

She was getting something out of the refrigerator, but she stopped, held the door open, and looked over at Nutty. "No, I *know* you're not dumb. In fact, I think you're much smarter than anyone realizes. I think you're smarter than *you* even know. You never push yourself, that's all. And I guess that's even okay. You won't have a heart attack when you're forty; you'll probably always be very happy. But you could do somewhat more with what you've got."

"I'm not very happy right now." His mouth was full with a last big bite. He also took his last big drink of juice. He swallowed, and let a little burp slip out.

Mom turned and gave him a dirty look, but she said, "Really? You're not happy? What's bothering you?"

"I don't want to be nutty. I'm tired of everybody laughing at the stuff I do. I want to be smart. But today William and I were talking about a science project I could do for the science fair, and I couldn't even understand what he was talking about."

"No one can understand William Bilks. And you don't have to be a genius to be happy, or to do some good things in life. I just think you could try a little harder, maybe study a little more."

"Yup. That's what I'm going to do. Apply myself. You're looking at a new man. Frederick Nutsell, the applied boy."

"Good. I'm glad to hear that. And now that

I've given you all this free advice, how about applying yourself to salad making? There's a head of lettuce right there on the counter."

"I can't, Mom. I've got to go read all I can about the atom and *quandum* mechanics and stuff like that. If I'm going to be smart from now on, I'd better start working on it right now."

Mr. Nutsell had come into the room, just as Nutty had begun to speak. "Come on, son," he said, "help your mother with the salad. Don't start making up excuses."

"I'm serious, Dad. I've decided I've got to start studying more. Mom and I talked it over, and I decided I'm going to start applying myself. I'm going to start living up to my potential—really make something of myself."

Nutty saw that old glow of excitement come into his dad's eyes, saw that he was buying this one.

"Well, son, that's wonderful. I'm thrilled to hear that. You know, I've been telling you all along, you're a young man with unlimited potential. It's just a matter of putting your talents to work, pushing yourself a little—striving to reach inside yourself to plumb your own depths."

"I think you're right, Dad. I haven't done enough plumbing in my depths."

"Son, I think the coaching I gave you during basketball season is starting to pay off. I think you've begun to discover what you're capable of."

"Me too. I'm going to go read the encyclopedia."

"Great, son. Just great. I'm proud of you."

"If you're so proud of him for getting out of making the salad, you make it," Mom said.

Dad got a look of panic in his eyes. "Oh, honey, I'm sorry. I was just going to read the newspaper. An insurance man really needs to keep up on what's—"

Nutty took the chance to clear out. He stopped in the living room and got the *A* volume of the encyclopedia, and went to his room.

He sat down on his bed and opened the big volume to the section on the atom. Maybe, if he stuck around William and picked up some of his study habits, he could be as smart as anyone at the lab school. Maybe he really could start applying himself, whatever that meant. He was really going to dig into this atomic stuff, and he would start by reading the encyclopedia right now.

Or at least right after dinner. He suddenly felt the need to stretch out and rest his weary mind.

After dinner, Nutty did give the encyclopedia another shot. The information was kind of interesting at first, but then the big words started piling up on each other and Nutty got lost. If only being smart were a little easier, it wouldn't be so bad.

He was glad when the phone rang and Susie

yelled down the hallway that it was for him. Nutty got up from his bed and went out to the kitchen. It was Orlando calling.

"Hey, Nutty, I was wondering—"

"My name's Frederick. Why don't you guys ever call me by my name?"

"What are you talking about? You threatened to kill me if I ever called you Frederick—or even told anyone what your real name was."

"I know. But I changed my mind. 'Nutty' makes me sound stupid."

"Right. It fits you."

"Lay off, Orlando. I'm smarter than you are."

"What? Smarter than me? I could out think you with my brain tied behind my back."

"That's a stupid thing to say, Orlando. I really hate to tell you that, but it's in a range I'd call mega-stupid." Nutty sat down on the kitchen floor and leaned against the wall. He stretched his long legs halfway across the kitchen, and crossed them at the ankles. "But then you can't help it. You do the best you can."

To Nutty's surprise, Orlando didn't respond to that one. Instead, he said, "Look, I gotta know something. Are you really taking this science project seriously? Are you really going to do something fancy?"

"Yeah. Why?"

"I don't know. I just thought you were laying it on thick. I've been thinking. Maybe I want to do something that won't take so much time. But if you're going to go all out, then I guess I have to."

"Then you have to."

"What are you going to do? Just give me some idea."

"All right. It has to do with atoms and the mechanics of quanthums. I'm going to try to figure out whether the little things inside atoms have brains, and whether—"

"What?"

"Yes. You heard right. It's something I've given a lot of thought to. Sometimes the little pieces of atoms do things that you can't figure out. They act like they have brains. So I'm going to—"

"What are you talking about, Nutty? How do you know that?"

"It's . . . just something I've noticed."

"Noticed? How can you notice something inside an atom?"

"Well, I don't mean I saw it. But I thought about it. And then I've been reading a bunch of stuff about atoms. I guess it's just sort of a hobby of mine now."

"Nutty, you're nuts."

"Actually, I don't let many people know about this, but I'm really pretty smart." For no particular reason he had wrapped the cord to the phone around his neck and was pretending to strangle himself.

"You don't let *anybody* know about it. You don't know beans about atoms, Nutty. How are you going to figure out if they have brains or not?"

"That part is secret. I'm going to do some experiments. I just can't tell you what. Do you even know what photons are?"

"Yeah. People from the planet Fote."

"Don't be ridiculous. They're things that float around in light."

"You mean that stuff you can see when—"

"No, no. Don't be stupid. That's just dust. I'm talking small stuff—millions and billions of times smaller than that. You really don't know enough for me to explain all this to you."

"Yeah, right." Orlando didn't sound much in a mood to kid around. He normally would have had a good answer.

"Wait a minute. William is helping you, isn't he?"

"What?" Nutty got up, cutting off circulation to his head in the process. He did a three-sixty to get himself undone. He was going to hang up just as quickly as he could think of an excuse.

"William is figuring this stuff out for you. I should have known."

"William's not *doing* it for me."

"He's in on it. I know he is. That's where you're picking up this stuff."

"Hey, scientists work in teams all the time. That's not anything new. Me and William are interested in some of the same kind of—"

"Geez, Nutty, that's rotten. You can't let William do your project for you."

"Hey, I'm not. All right? I'll be doing a lot of it on my own."

"Oh, sure."

"Well, I am. So get off my back." Nutty suddenly hung up the phone. He didn't need to listen to any more of this. Where did Orlando get off always making such accusations anyway?

The next day at school Nutty told Orlando—along with Richie and Bilbo—that he was a new person now. He was going to *apply* himself. The boys, for some reason, laughed at that. Orlando said he ought to apply for a new brain first. But little did they know about Nutty. Once he made his mind up—that brilliant mind that just hadn't ever been put to full use—there would be no stopping him. At least that's what Nutty told himself. All the same, that night at William's, Nutty found himself as baffled as ever.

"No, Nutty," William told him. "It has nothing to do with smashing atoms. We're not making a bomb, even if that's been your specialty in the past." And then he went into another lengthy explanation. It all had something to do with waves and particles and photons knowing where they were supposed to go—but Nutty couldn't imagine such a thing. Nutty was lying on his back on William's bed. He had his eyes shut, and he was trying with all his might to understand. "Are you saying these tiny things are like some kind of little animal or something? They fly around and land where they're supposed to?"

"No, they aren't animals, Nutty. But they seem to possess understanding. I told you, I can't explain that. No one can. That's what we're trying to do—see if we can't get some inkling of what's going on." William had been pacing, but now he stopped and leaned his back against the bookcase by his desk. "But if photons understand their role in the universe, maybe they understand the cosmic principles that give harmony to the billions of particles that form the planet. Photons seem to offer the best opportunity for us because particles of light travel in waves, and our brain has waves—and so does a magnet. We're going to try to bring all these waves into synchronization, and see whether we can touch on some form of communication."

"Hold it. Wait. I need to be able to explain this to people. Give me something I can say that a bunch of fifth graders will understand." Nutty closed his eyes tighter, and waited for the answer. He had to get this all straight.

"All right. Don't try to explain why we think that photons possess consciousness. Just say that it's a scientific theory. Tell them that we are trying to bring waves of light into the same pattern with your brain waves. It's just an experiment to see whether that will lead to some kind of communication between your consciousness and that of the photons in the light. It's that simple." William motioned outward with his hands, and then stuck them deep into his pockets.

Nutty opened his eyes and stared at the light fixture on the ceiling. "William, when I show up at the science fair, what am I going to take with me? That's what I don't get. Am I going to claim I've been talking with light waves, or am I going to have something I can show people?"

"Okay. Good questions. I've merely been trying to explain the theory behind all this. But you need to see the form the experiment will take. We can't really hope for any significant breakthrough between now and then, but at least you can show our experimental apparatus, and explain the philosophy that underlies our attempt."

"What if someone asks me a question?"

"You'll be fine. I think you'll start understanding this better as we go along."

"I hope so. Because I'm a mess right now."

William got up and walked to his closet and then pulled out a very strange-looking device. It was a wooden box, painted black, with a hinged lid and a large, round hole in one side. William set the box on the floor, and Nutty knelt to get a closer look. When he opened the lid, he could see that to the large hole William had attached the collar of a turtleneck shirt, also black, and he had cut a smaller hole on the side opposite the big one. "What's this for?" Nutty asked, pointing to the turtleneck.

"It provides a place for you to put your head through, but it will keep light from leaking out of the box."

William went back to his closet and came back with a small floodlight. He had equipped it with a rubber ring so that it would fit and hold tight in the smaller hole. "You will put your head into the box," he said, "and then we'll bombard your brain with photons from this light."

"Wait a minute, William. This is it? I'm going to go to the science fair and stick my neck through a hole in a wooden box and shine a light on my head?"

"Yes. Or someone else could demonstrate while you explain."

Nutty tipped over backward and lay flat on the carpet with arms spread out wide. "William, people are going to laugh. This is crazy."

"Not at all. For one thing, I will apply a magnetic field, with two large magnets on opposite sides of the box. You'll simply explain the idea: actual heat-sensitive photographs have shown that a magnetic field, passing through the head, will line up the hydrogen atoms in the brain. The method is being used as a new way of taking pictures of the brain— like the X-ray. Didn't you see those pictures in *National Geographic?*"

"I guess I missed that issue."

"That's too bad. I'll lend you my copy. It'll help you understand what I'm contriving. I'm simply theorizing that lining up the hydrogen atoms in the brain, then sending light waves through, might be some sort of key. Added to that, we'll experiment with various mental states, thus altering your brain waves until we find just the right combination that brings all those waves together."

"Maybe you ought to do this, William. I wouldn't know a photon if he stopped me on the street and asked me what time it was."

"No. I've thought about that. You're the one who learned the super concentration it took to play perfect basketball. We can use that concentration now for something infinitely more important. Besides, a simple mind may not wander as much as a more complex one tends to do."

"Thanks a lot."

"Well, I didn't mean to—"

"That's all right. But if we don't get any results,

this contraption looks nuts. I mean, a turtleneck? This thing looks like a portable tanning salon. No one will take it seriously."

"They will if you take it seriously and explain it right."

"No they won't, William. If you did it, they would. But no one takes me seriously."

"Well, they will someday. Let's not worry about that for now. Let's just get started."

William started hooking up the magnets. Nutty got out of the way. He couldn't believe this. He had heard that geniuses were usually crazy. Maybe that's what William was. Maybe he had finally drifted over the edge of the world and was swimming out in space somewhere.

"All right. Lie down and put your head through the hole."

Nutty really didn't want to do this, but he knew he had to. William would die if he didn't. So Nutty knelt down and crawled forward with his head down, like a hog rooting in the mud.

"No, no. Lie on your back, and I'll help you slide it over your head. You need to be in a restful, relaxed position."

"Have you got a pillow in there?"

"No. But that's an excellent thought, Nutty. You really should be comfortable. Next time I'll have a layer of foam rubber ready. But this time, let's try it without. I won't leave you in very long.

This is just a trial run to see whether everything is ready to go."

Nutty got on his back and stretched his neck, lifting his head off the floor, while William worked the turtleneck over his head. "Watch the ears," Nutty grumbled, but William paid no attention. He shut the lid, and all was dark for a few seconds. Then the light came on, blinding Nutty. "Hey, that's bright."

"Shut your eyes and relax."

"That light is hot."

"Oh—I hadn't thought about that. I may have to create a tube, and direct the light from a farther distance."

"Either that or I'll be bald before I turn twelve."

"Nutty, we'll work out the little flaws. Concentrate on our ultimate goal. Think about the moment when you make contact."

"How will I know?"

"I don't know. It's one of the things I've tried to imagine. I only trust that when your brain waves unite with the light waves, and the photons speak to the atoms of your brain, somehow, you'll know something. Maybe, you'll feel something you've never experienced before."

"Yeah, or I'll smell something strange when my brain starts to cook."

"Be still now. Relax. Try to focus your

thoughts. Let's just experiment with a few things."

"Those magnets won't pull my brains out of shape will they? I don't want to come out of here looking like some alien from the planet X."

"Nutty, hush. And don't make any more jokes."

"Jokes? Who's joking? I'm the guy with his head in the microwave."

"That's enough, all right? Let's try this. Think about trees—whole forests of beautiful trees, maybe on a beautiful hillside. Something like that. If you start to feel anything even slightly out of the ordinary, raise your hand."

Nutty tried, but the only thing he could think about was that light burning into the top of his head. He waited a good two minutes, and then he raised his hand.

William spoke softly, but with intensity. "Yes, yes. Speak. Tell me what you feel, but don't let your mind wander."

"I think my hair is on fire. Can't you smell it?"

"No. Now come on, Nutty. Picture something else. A beautiful little stream. Clear, cold water whispering as it flows over a pretty little waterfall."

But Nutty saw himself in a desert, and the sun, huge and hot, was burning him to a crisp. He didn't dare say so. In fact, he didn't dare say anything. Eventually William whispered, "Nutty, do you have it? Do you have the vision?"

37

"No."

"Why not?"

"How can I think of fresh water when I've got salt water running into my eyes?"

"Okay, okay." William popped the box open. "Slide your head out. We'll have to make some adjustments so you won't get so hot inside. That's just the sort of thing we had to learn this time. But Nutty, if you're going to joke and complain all the time, we have no hope at all."

Nutty was still sliding the contraption off his head when he heard another voice. As his eyes adjusted, he realized that Orlando had come into the room.

"What's going on?" he said.

William jumped up. "What are you doing here?"

"Your mom told me to come down, that you guys were here. What's that thing?"

"What do you want?"

"Well, I figured since you were helping Nutty on his project, maybe you could help me with mine."

"Not right now, Orlando. We're busy."

"What is that thing? Is that your project, Nutty?"

"Yes. But don't tell anyone what it is."

"How could I? I don't *know* what it is."

William got up from where he had been kneeling. "I don't mind telling you, if you'll keep it to yourself. Briefly stated, Orlando, we are attempting to commune with sub-atomic particles. It's highly experimental, but well worth the effort. We hope to bring Nutty's brain waves into harmony with photons of light."

"Nutty has brain waves? Are you sure?"

"Orlando, this is serious."

"Yeah, I know. Nutty tried to tell me about it. But I don't get what the box is for."

"Nutty puts his head inside the box, and I apply both a magnetic field and a stream of light. We hope to bring the particles of light into contact with the atoms in Nutty's brain."

"And you're going to do this at the science fair?"

"Yes."

"Nutty, you're going to slip your head through that turtleneck, and stick your head between two magnets while William shines light on your brain?"

Nutty nodded, tentatively, watching for Orlando's reaction.

But he showed none. He nodded a couple of times, as though he were quite interested. Finally, he said, "Do you care if I just make one comment?"

"Not at all," William said.

Orlando nodded a couple more times, seriously, and then he said, "Here's what I think." He suddenly dropped on the floor and started laughing in wild fits.

"You're not funny," Nutty said.

William was not amused either. He told Orlando to show some respect or get lost. But Orlando couldn't do either.

Nutty knew what to expect at school the next morning, but it started a little sooner than he thought it would. When he walked through the door into Mrs. Smiley's class, Orlando said, "Here he is now—Frankenstein's monster."

The way everyone laughed, Nutty had no doubt that Orlando had already told them about the black box. "Hey, Nutty," Richie said, "I understand you have a new outfit you're wearing these days—a nice turtleneck box."

Nutty gave Richie a cold stare for a moment, and then said, "It's usually people who understand the least who are the first to open their mouths and prove it." It was a line Nutty had worked on ahead of time. He knew he was going to catch a lot of flak today.

But Orlando and Richie only laughed harder. "I heard it's really a sauna for the head," Orlando said. "It's for people who have fat heads but thin bodies—like you, Nutty."

Nutty took a quick glance at Sarah; unfortunately, she seemed to be enjoying all this. "Orlando," Nutty said, quietly, walking over close to him, "if you want all your limbs to stay connected to your body, you'll shut your mouth right now."

"I guess you scientific types like to pull things apart and see what makes them work, huh?"

"That's right. In your case, I just might open up your head and try to discover why intelligent life cannot survive there."

Nutty didn't wait for a reply; he walked around to his desk and plopped down. He sat straight across from Orlando, but with a row of desks in between them. He watched out of the corner of his eye. Orlando had turned and was talking to Richie, who sat even farther away from Nutty. The two of them were laughing.

If Nutty had been sure that the science project would work out and that the guys would have to swallow their pride and say so, Nutty could have enjoyed all this. But as it was, he just figured that everyone would make fun of the whole idea—even after they had seen it.

Bilbo leaned over and said, "What is this thing you're doing? Has William gone nuts or something?"

Nutty didn't even have a chance to answer because Mrs. Smiley had stood up and was about to get things started. But at recess later that morning, Bilbo stopped Nutty as they walked outside, and he asked again, "What's the deal with the box and the light? Orlando said you came out of the thing all sweaty—like William was trying to cook your brain or something."

"It's not for heat," Nutty said. "It's for light. William wants my brain waves to start flowing right—that's what the magnets are for—and mix in with the light waves. I'm supposed to start understanding all those little things that are in light—called photons—or they're supposed to understand me, or something like that."

"What?"

Nutty heard giggling, and he turned around. Sarah had come out of the school behind them, and she had been listening in. "Nutty, that's the craziest thing I've ever heard. Why do you let William talk you into these things?"

"He didn't do it all. We're partners. We're

both going to be scientists. If we ever make this thing work, we'll be famous for it."

"Come on, Nutty. A box with a light shining on your head? William must have let you think this one up on your own."

"So what's that supposed to mean? That I'm stupid?" Nutty's voice sounded angry.

Sarah seemed to realize that she had pushed Nutty a little too hard. "Hey, I didn't mean anything."

"Do you ever?" Nutty said, and he walked away. But he knew immediately that he had done something stupid—partly because he knew he had said something mean, and partly because he was walking across the playground, with everyone watching, and without the slightest idea where he was going.

By the time Nutty got to William's house that night, he had decided to withdraw from the whole deal. He would have to think up some project that would save face somehow. But when he told William that, William's patience seemed to hit the breaking point.

"Nutty, what do you care what everyone thinks? Those people don't have the brains to judge what we're doing. They don't have the first notion about such things. Do you really think you should throw over one of the great experiments in the history of the world because *Orlando* doesn't understand it? By that standard no one would ever do much of *anything.*"

Nutty was lying on the floor. He wasn't preparing to put on the box; he was just relaxing. All day he had been mad at his friends for being so stupid, but now, suddenly, he didn't like what William was saying. "William, Orlando's probably about as smart as I am. He does about as well as I do in school. Richie's pretty close too. And Bilbo and Sarah are both smarter than me."

"Than I."

"No, they're not as smart as you."

"No. I mean you should say 'smarter than I.'"

"No way, William. I'm not anywhere near as smart as you."

"Nutty, I know that. I'm simply correcting your grammar."

"But you don't think I'm near as smart as you?"

"Nearly."

"I'm nearly as smart as you?"

"No, of course not. But you should say 'nearly as smart,' not 'near as smart.' Grammar again."

Nutty had to think that all back through. What had they just said? He stared at the light fixture.

"I don't get it, William. You don't need me. You could get a rat to put his head in that box."

"No. Of course not." William stood up again, and he looked over at the pictures of his heroes, the philosophers. "It must be a human. It must be some-one who can understand and articulate what we learn. And I want it to be a good friend—someone I can share everything with."

"Okay. That's all right with me. But couldn't you help me rig up one of those little demonstra-tions on erosion—just run some water over dirt—or something like that? I could put that in the science fair, and we could keep our mouths shut about all this other stuff until we get some real results."

"Well, maybe. Let's think about that. But for now, let's give it another shot. I want to introduce sound waves tonight—music—as a way of helping you relax and channel your thoughts."

"Okay. I guess you want me to put that hot box on my head now." He raised his head, as if ready to have William slide it on.

"Yes, but I've modified it. Look at the exten-sion I've added." William had found a tube, and had stuck that in the small hole, and to that he had at-tached the floodlight.

"That ought to help," Nutty said, but that wasn't what he was thinking. He told himself, "There's no way in the world I'm going to end up chatting with photons—music or no music, magnet or no magnet." What would he say anyway? "Hello, there. I'm Nutty Nutsell. I just stuck my head in to say hello. How about the weather we've been hav-ing in this box lately?"

But Nutty slipped his head through the turtleneck, not admitting his doubts to William. He immediately felt the soft foam rubber that William had applied to the bottom of the box. With less heat and a softer resting place, Nutty felt much better. He didn't expect any results, but at least he wouldn't suffer.

William put on the music. It was something gentle and classical, and as far as Nutty was concerned, boring. But it did sound something like the scene William began to describe.

"You are resting by a lovely blue lake. Across the lake are majestic snowcapped mountains, which reflect in the placid water. A forest of green pine trees lines the shore. You rise and go to your boat, get in, push off, and then, lie back and drink in all this beauty. The boat is rocking ever so slightly; the breeze is soft and cool, and it touches your hair like the touch of a loving hand."

Nutty sort of liked that. It reminded him of a commercial he had seen on TV. Except William had left out this gorgeous girl with dark hair and—

"Concentrate on the vision, Nutty. You feel yourself at one with all this beauty: sky, earth, water, all blended into a perfect picture of tranquility."

Don't forget the girl, William.

"As the boat drifts, you look up into the deep blue of the sky against those craggy cliffs and white fields of snow. And you feel yourself drawn away from the petty concerns of simple daily life."

Nutty couldn't help smiling. This was all sort of stupid. And yet, he *was* feeling the rocking of the boat, the gentle breezes. He liked the feeling, liked the thought of floating aimlessly across those waters. The music was also moving through him, though he was hardly aware of it. Somehow the picture in his mind, the touch of the air, the sense of well-being, the caressing sound of music and wind in the trees, and the lapping of the water—even the girl William had left out—had become mixed into one sensation, and it was nice.

"Ever so gradually the scene dissolves into something finer. You rise from the water and float in air and time. And yet there is no air, no water, no time. You are part of all things, and all things are part of you."

Nutty felt himself drifting now. The mountains and trees had disappeared, the water lost its motion. All was sensation—pure and perfect. He was lost in bright, glowing timelessness. He wanted to hang there now, free of the real world, free even of himself, and—

"Nutty."

and—

"Nutty!"

and—

48

"Nutty, for crying out loud, did you fall asleep?"

"What?" The glow was suddenly gone. Nutty opened his eyes and saw nothing, total darkness. "What's going on?"

"You fell asleep in the middle of our experiment."

"No, I didn't. I was sort of . . ."

"Sort of asleep. You didn't even hear me at first."

Nutty pulled his head out of the box. He didn't like the light in the room.

"Nutty, I'm very disappointed in you. I don't think you're taking this whole thing seriously."

Nutty shrugged. Maybe he *had* gone to sleep. If so, it was a nice dream. He wished William had left him alone. And yet, something strange had happened—some brightness had crept into his mind, and there, for a moment, he had been on the edge of something. He wondered if maybe the experiment had begun to work.

"Look, William, I have to get home. I promised my parents I'd be home before nine."

"That's fine. But Nutty, if we're going to have any hope of getting anywhere with this thing, you have to concentrate. You can't let your mind drift away."

"It didn't drift away, William. I was thinking about all that stuff, and then I just sort of . . ."

"Fell asleep."

"I guess so."

"Well, maybe it was all too serene. We'll have to try lots of different mental states."

"Yeah. I guess." Nutty got up and put on his jacket. But something was bothering him. "William,

I really felt kind of strange there at the end. I didn't think I was asleep."

"Well, you were just drifting off, I suppose."

"Maybe, but there was this glowing in my mind. Hey, by the way, why did you turn the light off?"

"Because we were finished."

"No, I mean, before we were finished. When I opened my eyes, everything was black inside the box."

William was still kneeling by the box. He looked puzzled. "That's not possible. The light was still on at that point."

"No, William. I'm sure about that. The box was black inside."

William suddenly looked very strange. He had that look he always got when he thought he was on to something, his eyes narrowing and piercing right through Nutty. He turned to the box, hesitated, and then lifted the lid very slowly. "Good heavens," he whispered.

Nutty knelt down beside him, and they peered into the box, but there was nothing to see. All was dark—completely black. The light from the fixture on the ceiling—almost directly above the box—failed to penetrate even slightly into the darkness.

"What the heck's going on, William?"

"The box is empty of all light. We're looking at absolute darkness."

"But why doesn't it fill up again? The light ought to shine into it."

"I know. But it doesn't. I have no idea how to explain it." William shut the top and opened it again, but all remained dark inside.

"We must have done something weird, William."

"Nutty, it's more than some clever little trick. The laws of physics are being defied before our eyes. Nothing like this has ever happened before—never in the history of the entire world!"

"Wow. What a science project!"

"What?"

"I can show this box at the science fair, and tell Orlando and all those guys to take a good long look at absolute darkness and see whether they think that's a hot enough project for them."

The two boys were kneeling on opposite sides of the box. William looked at Nutty with eyes full of wonder. "Nutty, you're still not seeing the significance of what has happened here. This is something a whole lot bigger than an elementary-school science fair. This is some sort of breakthrough. We have to try to figure out what it means."

Nutty sat back and tried to think. But he had no inkling as to what they had done. The truth was—no matter what William said—he was a lot more excited to have something good for the science fair. He could see it all. "You see before you a box empty of all light. Go ahead, shine your flashlights into it. Notice how the light stops, unable to penetrate absolute darkness. And please, Orlando, Bilbo, and Richie, eat my shorts."

"Nutty, can you stay here all night? I'd like to try some other things—or at least discuss this from every angle."

"Actually, William, I was supposed to be home by now. Maybe we can work on it tomorrow night. Now that we at least have something we can show people, maybe we can write up some signs or something that explains a little of what we did."

"All right. Go ahead." William's tone was suddenly less than patient. He got up and paced away from Nutty, his hands behind his back, like some old philosopher. "I might as well have the time alone anyway. I have to try to deal with this. If you're not interested, you wouldn't be of any help."

"Hey, I'm interested. It's just that . . . well, you know my parents. They'd think I was making a big deal out of nothing. But I'll stop over tomorrow night, if I can."

William nodded, but he was lost in thought. Nutty walked out the door. "Oh, Nutty, wait." William followed him into the dark hallway. "Don't tell anyone about this yet. Not anyone at all, including your parents. We can't let this get around until we've verified what we have and can present it in a clear way. In fact, we might want to wait until—*oh, my goodness!*"

"What's the matter?"

"Oh my . . . *GOODNESS!*"

Nutty had never heard William sound quite so scared, or shocked, or startled, or whatever he was.

"William, what are you—"

"Come back to my bedroom—quickly."

Nutty was suddenly scared himself. William wasn't one to lose his cool, but at the moment he sounded as though he had just seen a ghost.

"Stand in front of that mirror, Nutty. Look at yourself. Do you see anything strange?"

"Strange? Like what?"

"Okay, you don't see it yet. I can't see it in here either. But now I'm going to turn off the light. Keep looking in the mirror, and tell me what you see."

William switched off the light, and for a moment Nutty's eyes didn't adjust. He saw nothing at all. And then, ever so slowly, he saw a light—a subtle, golden sort of glow—all around his face and head.

"Hey, what's going on?"

"I'm not sure."

"Well, get it off me, will you? What the heck is it anyway?"

"I don't know. The light that used to be in the box, I guess."

"What are you talking about, William? Light doesn't do that. Get it off me. You've made me radioactive or something."

"I don't think so, Nutty. I don't think it will hurt you."

"You don't *think.* Hey, thanks a lot. For all you know, my brain could be getting fried right now. Geez, William, what have we done?"

"Calm down, Nutty." William flipped the light on. "You're okay. I'm pretty sure that the photons have collected around your head. They've chosen to stay near you rather than to stay in the box." William was starting to sound excited. "Nutty, I think we've got something. I think we've made some kind of incredible discovery. I think we've made contact with the inner world." His hands had gradually risen into the air, and then in utter joy, he clapped the sides of his head. "This is too marvelous to believe."

"Oh sure, that's easy for you to say. You're not the one with the glow-in-the-dark face. For all you know, those little photon dudes could be mad at me. They might be getting ready to slice my brain up with lasers."

"They're not little people, Nutty. They're just particles. But I've been telling you they have a will of their own. They've chosen you; they've become compatible with your mental state. I think they want to stay with you. Maybe they even want to communicate with you."

"Okay. Here's some communication. Get lost, you little runts. Get out of my face." Nutty started rubbing his head and face wildly, and then knocked his knuckles against his skull. "Get lost, do you hear me? Get away from me."

"Nutty, don't. Anger might scare them away. Don't lose this chance." He grabbed Nutty's wrists, and held them tight. "Just relax, and don't panic. This is the most important moment of our lives. Don't ruin it."

"Right. But do you have any bug spray?"

"Nutty, I'm serious."

"So am I. If you think I'm going to go around shining like a lamppost the rest of my life, you're crazy."

"Nutty, there's no telling how long they'll stay. You may have scared them off already. For right now, we have to try to learn what there is to learn."

But Nutty had grabbed on to the idea that they were already gone. He flipped the light off, and then hurried back to the mirror, crashing into William's chair as he moved through the dark. When he got to the mirror, however, the glow was still there, and the longer he waited, the more clearly he could see it. His face shone softly, and around his head, maybe two inches thick, was a gentle, amber illumination, like the glow around the moon on an overcast night.

"I look like a stoplight, William. I'm going to

stop traffic. People are going to think I'm some sort of man from outer space."

"Don't exaggerate, Nutty. It's a soft light. People will only see it if you get in a dark place."

"Oh, sure. Forget about movies, right? Forget about camping out. Forget about ever taking a girl out in my whole life. 'Sorry, Sarah, I have to be in by seven. You see, I glow in the dark.'"

"No, no. Don't look at it that way. This may be a brief experience. We have to get what we can from it. Or, if it lasts, you'll be famous."

Nutty stood there in the dark, wondering whether he liked that idea. But it scared him. "I don't want to be famous, William. Not for having a 'light' complexion. I want to be normal."

"But you've been telling me you want to be smart."

"How many smart people glow when you turn the lights off, William? Tell me that. This has nothing to do with being smart."

"All right, now listen." William stepped closer to Nutty in the dark. "I want you to stop this. I want you to go home and get a good night's rest. I'm not sure what we should do next. I'll think this all through. We just need to decide on a plan. In the meantime, don't tell anyone what's happened."

"Tell? I don't have to tell. If someone turns out a light, I turn into a neon sign."

"Don't let that happen. Avoid people on the

way home and especially your parents—except in a fully lighted room. The same with your little sister. And avoid any darkness, even a dimly lighted hallway at school tomorrow. By tomorrow night, I'll have a plan worked out. We'll be announcing this to the world before long, but—"

"The world? What do you mean, William? I don't want *the world* to know about me looking like this." Nutty was staring into the mirror, and it seemed to him that the glow was growing brighter.

"Don't be selfish, Nutty. You'll be one of the most famous people alive before long. Frederick Nutsell and William Bilks—the men who broke through to the sub-atomic world. Columbus will be nothing compared to us. Neil Armstrong will be someone out of the Dark Ages."

"Yeah, well, I'm going to end the Dark Ages, all right. I'm the cutest little night-light that ever came along."

William flipped the light back on. "No, Frederick. You're a light in the dark to a world struggling to understand the deepest mysteries. We've stepped into a new world, and for you, there's no turning back now."

"Oh, brother." Nutty touched his face, rubbed his hands over his hair, trying to see whether he felt strange in any way. "William, I don't need all this. All I wanted was a nice little project for the science fair."

When Nutty went to bed that night he was nervous
and worried. He had just slipped under the covers
when he heard his mother coming down the hall.
He jumped up and turned on his light, and then he
grabbed the encyclopedia and pretended to be reading. She stepped in and said it was really time to get
to sleep. He promised her that he was going to turn
the light off soon. He really wanted to talk to her
about the mess William had gotten him into, but he
knew she would worry.

When he did turn the light off, he was restless.
He wasn't even sure that photons were the cause of
the glowing. It was fine for William to think so, but
how did Nutty know it wasn't some weird medical

problem? Maybe the lamp had cloned him or something; maybe he was going to grow up to be a giant floodlight.

But slowly, he relaxed. A gradual quiet came over him, and his mind settled into a rather nice, comfortable state. It wasn't so much that he decided everything was all right; in fact, the feeling wasn't much like thought at all. He merely drifted into something like sleep, except that his consciousness seemed heightened rather than diminished. A golden haze filled his vision, within his closed eyes, and his body seemed suspended in space. His senses perceived no bed, no room, no darkness; the lovely, warm glow became everything.

Nutty felt that he never slept that night, that he simply slid into a translucent space where all was right. And yet, the night passed quickly, and as the sunrise brought gradual light into the room, just as gradually he became aware of the real world around him. He had never felt so relaxed, so at peace, in his life.

Nutty got out of bed a little earlier than usual, walked calmly to the bathroom, and took a shower that felt like a glorious, warm massage. The scent of the soap and shampoo was so sweet that it almost made him swoon. He dressed for school and was ready earlier than usual. When his mother called him to breakfast, he went immediately, not waiting for the fourth or fifth call, the way he usually did.

He sat down at the kitchen table, but he didn't speak. He felt the warm glow of light in the kitchen, liked the serenity, the velvet touch of the air, the exquisite aroma of pancakes. It seemed, for some reason, the loveliest moment of his life, and yet, he didn't say any such words to himself. He merely drank in the sensations.

"What's with you this morning?" Mom said. Nutty slowly turned and looked at her. He wondered what she meant. "You look like you're still half asleep."

"No. I'm not."

"Are you okay?"

"I feel wonderful, Mother, absolutely wonderful. I can't think of words to describe how . . . wonderful . . . I feel."

Mom took a curious glance at him, and then laughed. "Well, I guess that's what love does to you."

"Love?"

"Hey, I get my reports from the lab school. I hear that Sarah Montag has a big crush on you. Is that right?"

"Yes. That's true."

"And what do you think of her?"

"I love her."

Mom had been attending to the breakfast, but now she turned toward Nutty. "Freddie! You're joking, aren't you?"

"No."

"You never said anything like that about a girl before. You mean you like her, don't you?"

"I love her. And I love Bilbo and Orlando and Richie. I love everyone at my school. I love you too. And Dad. And little Susie."

Mom broke up. "Oh, Freddie, you have the weirdest sense of humor. I never know what to expect from you."

Nutty didn't answer, didn't laugh. He was glowing inside and out, wrapped in the loveliness of a spring morning. And then he felt pain, sadness, and was suddenly deeply disturbed. He turned toward the window and looked outside.

Mom was calling to Dad and Susie to come to breakfast, and Nutty heard her words, but he was fully captured by what he saw and felt.

When Dad came into the kitchen, he sat down and said, "Good morning, Freddie. What are you looking at?"

"Dad, the grass and the trees are hurting. The carbon monoxide from all the cars is causing them stress. Could you feed them today? Some fertilizer would mean so much to them."

"What?"

"I'm not sure what this is," Mom said. "He's doing some 'great philosopher' routine on us this morning. He just told me that he loved us all—even Susie."

Susie had just come into the room. "Yuck," she said. "He better not tell *me* that or I'll sock him in the nose."

Susie sat down and Nutty turned toward her. "I must have hurt your feelings sometime," he said. "In fact, I know I have. I'm very, very sorry."

He reached for Susie, and tried to wrap his arms around her, but she pushed him away and jumped off her chair. "Would you lay off?" she said.

"Yeah, Freddie, come on," Dad said. "That's about enough of that routine."

"Leave him alone," Mom said. "If he wants to act like he likes his little sister, I'll take that over the usual stuff we get around here."

But Nutty was feeling the pain of his little sister's rejection. He hated to think that she felt no more love for him. And he felt for the trees too. The poor trees and grass. They were aching. Nutty had never known that kind of pain.

At school that morning Nutty greeted his friends, calmly and warmly, but was confused by their teasing. It seemed so harsh and unkind. He went to his seat, saddened. And yet, when Mrs. Smiley said hello and smiled, he was suddenly transported to glorious happiness. "Mrs. Smiley," he said, "thank you. You make me feel so welcome and so happy. I love you very much."

The class gave out a sort of collective gasp, and

everyone spun around to look at Nutty. And then the laughing began. When Nutty didn't laugh, this only cracked the others up all the more. "Nutty, that's not really funny," Mrs. Smiley said, and then she smiled. She had long since given up on trying to call him Frederick or Freddie. "But thanks anyway."

Nutty could see that she thought he was joking. He wondered why she didn't trust his feelings. He knew that he had not always been as kind to her as he should have been—had even said unkind things about her to the other boys—but he wanted to change that now.

Nutty worked on his math that morning with wonderful satisfaction. He saw the way the numbers related, understood the concepts as he never had before. Each time he computed the correct answer, he thrilled to the rightness of it. Math was so pure, so satisfying, like a game, and yet it was part of all things, too.

But something else began to press its way into his consciousness. He thought the shrubs, just outside the windows, were moaning softly. Finally, he had to give up his selfish pleasure with the numbers and go to them. He arose and walked to an open window. He reached out and touched the leaves, wiped away the dust from some of them. "I'm sorry," he said. "I'll try to help you."

"Nutty, what are you doing? Finish your math."

"I will, in a minute, ma'am. But I'm worried about these poor shrubs. So many cars come by here. They choke these innocent creatures with their exhaust. These shrubs would give anything for fresher air, a little more sunlight, a little more magnesium in the soil."

The kids were all laughing, but Mrs. Smiley wasn't. "Nutty, enough is enough. All right? I know you think you're very funny this morning, but I want you to sit down and do your work."

"I'm serious, Mrs. Smiley. It's not just these poor shrubs. We're cutting off the air they need; we're breaking down the ozone layer; we're dumping toxins into the soil they feed in. And think of the poor, dear soil. It never hurt anyone; it has given us all we have, and what do we give back to it but chemicals that burn and torture it? The soil is crying out, Mrs. Smiley, and the sands of our polluted seas are aching. They depend on us; they give to us. All they want is to be in harmony with us."

The kids were still laughing, but sort of nervously, as though they weren't sure he was kidding. And as the laughing died down, everyone kept staring at Nutty as though he had lost his mind. Mrs. Smiley took some time to respond. "Well, that's certainly true. You make a good point. We all must be more protective of our environment. I'm not sure whether you're trying to be funny or not, Nutty. I do know that I want you to sit down."

Nutty heard something in Mrs. Smiley's voice, a certain impatience that was painfully unfriendly. He was suddenly confused, and for the first time that morning he had some sense that everything was strange. Everyone was looking at him, and he could sense that they were not accepting his words, or his emotions. It pained him to see them pulling back, doubting him. But he was not himself, it finally occurred to him. Some of the golden aura that had filled his brain seemed to fade, and Nutty found himself wondering what had been going on.

"Nutty, I'm not going to ask you again," Mrs. Smiley said. "Now please sit down."

Nutty went to his seat. He looked around, and now the room was changed. He heard Mindy, the girl who sat in front of him, say, "He's just trying to show off. I think he's trying to pretend he's a brain, or something—probably because everyone's been teasing him about his science project. He can't pull off that kind of act with us though; we've known him too long."

The words hurt Nutty deeply. Tears began to flow down his cheeks. Those around him were staring again, but Nutty didn't care. He let the tears run down his face, and he felt that the pain was more than he could bear.

Sarah sat one row over and a couple of seats ahead of Nutty. She had turned and was staring at him now with her mouth wide open. "He's crying,"

Nutty heard her whisper. She seemed concerned. This warmed Nutty a little.

"Oh, Sarah, thank you," he said. "I'm glad you care about me." Nutty had spoken softly, but everyone around him heard.

A couple of kids sputtered with laughter, but Mindy said, "You gotta be kidding."

Bilbo leaned over and said, "Hey, Nutty, are you okay?"

Nutty felt the kindness, the concern, of his wonderful friend, and suddenly he was lifted to heights of joy. This good person cared about him. "Oh, thank you, Bilbo. You're such a dear, dear person—the finest friend a young man could ever have."

Bilbo looked at him like he had just lost his mind, and Mindy twisted around in her seat. "Have you been playing in the street or something? We better start looking for the hit-and-run driver."

Nutty was shocked and confused. He had never felt such friction before. Everything was so strange. People were not reacting as honestly and warmly as they really should. And at the same time Nutty knew within himself that his own behavior—even the powerful emotions he was feeling—were somehow not his usual feelings.

When lunchtime came, Nutty slipped away. He went out to the trees and the grass. He talked to the plants, promised them that he would do what he could for them. He noticed a patch of grass that was struggling to come to life but was not getting much moisture. He found a discarded cup in the trash barrel and carried water to the grass, making several trips from the fountain.

All this gave him pleasure, and yet, he could not rid himself of the gnawing feeling that he was acting strangely. Why didn't he want to be with his friends? Why had he never cared about the grass before? The pure joy of the early morning was gone, and yet, he could not bring himself to go about the day in his usual way.

That afternoon Nutty protected himself by keeping his mouth shut and staying within himself. He was still trying to understand what was happening. When school was out, he went back to the little patch of grass, talked to it, and promised to bring it water every day. And then he wandered down to the sand box that the kindergartners played in. It was empty now, and the sand had collected sun all day. Nutty took off his shoes, plunged his feet into the warmth and friendliness of the grains, and ran his fingers through the smoothness. "Sand," he said, "it's good to be here with you. I've never thanked you for all the pleasure you've given me in my life."

And then he heard a voice. "Nutty, what the heck are you doing? You're supposed to be at the Student Council meeting. It's starting right now. Everyone's looking for you."

"Orlando, sit down and take your shoes off. Enjoy the sand."

"Nutty, this isn't funny anymore. You're acting wacko. What's going on?"

"I'm not sure. I feel good—but I feel strange. I don't know what's happening to me."

"Does this have something to do with that stuff you and William are working on?" Orlando came around and sat down next to Nutty.

Suddenly Nutty knew. For the first time, he remembered what had happened the night before. "Yes, I think so. William and I did our experiment last night, and the photons collected around me. They must still be with me. My brain waves must be in harmony with them."

"Nutty, that's stupid. Those things can't come out of a floodlight and start following you around."

"They did, Orlando. We saw them. They collected around my head. William says it's a great scientific breakthrough."

"Oh, brother. It's William who's got you all messed up, not any crotons, or whatever those things are. He must have hypnotized you or something."

Nutty stood up, gathered up his shoes and socks, and said, "Come with me." He walked toward the school.

"Where are you going? You aren't supposed to go in there without shoes."

"Just come with me. I have to show you something." Nutty walked in through a back door to the school and down the hallway to the boys' room. He told Orlando to look at him closely, and then he reached over and switched off the light.

"What are you doing, Nutty?" Orlando said.

"Just look at me. Let your eyes get used to the dark."

"What are you talking about? I don't—" Suddenly Orlando let out a piercing scream.

The scream startled Nutty. He jumped back and cracked his head against the wall. Pain shot through his skull, and he grabbed the back of his head. At the same moment his mind jumped, and everything was completely changed. The glow inside his head, the comfort, was gone.

Orlando reached over and turned on the light. "Nutty, are you okay? I didn't mean to—"

"I'm okay. But how did we get here?"

"You brought me in here to show me those protons, or whatever they are. Man, they're all over your head, Nutty. You gotta do something."

It all came back. He remembered his whole day, but only in a dreamy haze. Things around him now suddenly seemed shockingly clear and sharp-edged. "I've been acting really weird, haven't I?"

"Yeah, man. You told Mrs. Smiley you loved her and—"

"Oh, wow. I did, didn't I?"

"Yeah, and you were out there talking to the sand, Nutty. I'm not kidding you. I came out there and you were telling the sand grains what a great bunch of guys they were."

Nutty was nodding. He remembered. And the memory was basically good. Yet it was frightening. "What are people saying about me?"

"They think you went off the high dive the wrong way—and landed on the concrete."

"Those photons are messing me up."

"No kidding, man. I think they want to move into your head and settle down."

"We've gotta get rid of them, Orlando. If I keep acting the way I did today, someone's going to throw a butterfly net over me and drag me away."

"Maybe they're gone now. You're acting okay." Orlando switched the light back off, and waited a second or two. "No way. You're lighting up like a firefly."

"Orlando, we've got to do something."

Orlando turned the light on again. "Right. But how can we get rid of the little suckers?"

"Maybe they like all that nice stuff I've been

saying. Let's talk mean, and loud, and mad. Maybe they'll run from that kind of talk."

Orlando suddenly gave Nutty a pretty good slap to the side of the head. "Hey, get lost, you little jerks. We hate your kind around here. Take a hike, do you hear me?"

Nutty was not overly happy about the shot he had taken, but he gave himself a few slaps of his own. "Yeah, get out of here. I hate you. You're driving me nuts."

Both boys were slapping and yelling now, thinking up anything bad they could call the photons. "You little green slime balls," Orlando yelled. "Go hang out with your own kind of gunk."

"You dirty little sleaze bits. You chunks of muck. Get off me. You're nothing but armpit sweat."

"Slugs. Garbage mouths. Hair balls."

"Slobber mouths. Sludge. Cow pies."

"We hate everything about you." Whack. Orlando gave Nutty another good shot to the side of the head. "You're ugly." Whack. "You're stupid." Whack. "You're a bunch of rejects." Whack. "We don't want to play with you. Don't come over to our house anymore." Whack.

"Okay, okay," Nutty finally said. "Hit *them*, not me."

"Let's see if they're gone." Orlando reached

over and turned off the light again, and Nutty stepped toward the mirror. For a moment he felt a twinge of hope, but then he saw the glow, and at the same time Orlando said, "Geez, man, that's scary. You look like a spaceman. Don't go for a walk at night. You'll scare all the little kids in your neighborhood."

"What am I going to do?"

"What about a swirly?"

"Lay off, Orlando. I'm not sticking my head in any toilet."

"It might be worth it. Even those things have got to hate a swirly."

Nutty was thinking. If he held his breath, maybe . . . no way. He was not sticking his head in a toilet, photons or not.

And then the door swung open. "Say, what's going on in here? What's all the yelling?" It was Mr. Skinner, the custodian. The light came on. "Oh, I might have known it would be you two. What do you think you're doing?"

"Just our daily hygiene, Mr. Skinner," Orlando said. "We were trying to scare the foo-tons off Nutty's head. It's something most people do every day. You can't get them all by shampooing."

"What?"

"Never mind. It's something we learned in health class. It's just part of proper personal care. I guess you didn't get any of that when you were in school."

Orlando walked out, past Mr. Skinner, and Nutty followed. Mr. Skinner was shaking his head and mumbling something about the boys being a couple of crackpots. And then when he saw that Nutty was carrying his shoes, he demanded that he put them on. "What were you guys planning to do, stop up the sinks and go wading?"

"No, sir," Orlando said. "But it's not a bad idea. Thanks for the suggestion."

"Yeah, you try it, and you'll answer to me." He walked into the boys' room, probably to check the sinks. Nutty sat down and put on his shoes and socks, and then he and Orlando went on down to the Student Council meeting. Everyone was getting ready to leave, and Mrs. Ash was very put out with Nutty. As president, Nutty was supposed to conduct the meeting.

Nutty told everybody to sit down, however, and he got the meeting going immediately. After reading the minutes, the first order of business was a committee report on the ongoing proposal to improve the food in the cafeteria. This was something Nutty had been very concerned about; it was his most important campaign promise, and the one he hadn't made enough progress on. But as Angela Vanghent, the committee chairperson, made her presentation, Nutty found himself having trouble paying attention. He was soon resting comfortably, but the touch of the chair was disappearing. He was slowly rising into golden space, it seemed, into quiet peace; and the feeling was so satisfying, that he couldn't resist.

Nutty was moved by the words of this lovely girl who had worked so hard to improve food for everyone. By the time she had stopped talking, Nutty moved slowly to the front of the room again and said, "Angela, I am so pleased with the work you have done. You must care very much about the universe to devote yourself this way."

A couple of guys laughed, but most people were glancing around to see what the others thought. Nutty could see their confusion. "I'm sorry," he said. "I know you don't expect such sentiments from me. I'm sorry for that. I hope I will be more sensitive to all your needs in the future."

Orlando stood up. *"Nutty,"* he yelled, stunning everyone. "Remember. You hate those little pus bags."

"Orlando!" Mrs. Ash said. "What a terrible thing to say."

"Oh, I didn't mean the kids. I meant the photo-tons, or whatever they are."

"It's all right," Nutty said. He was back, more or less, and he was struggling to stay that way. "I'm okay." By now everyone was really confused. But

Nutty pushed on, hoping to avoid any further talk of photons and the like. "We need to decide what action to take. I believe the food committee has a motion it would like to present."

Angela stood up again, and she made her motion. Nutty called for a second to the motion, and then allowed discussion. But the discussion gave him time to drift again, and the warmth began to seep into his brain and spread out through his body.

And then the pain hit him like a slam in the ribs. "Oh, students, we must do something," he said. "The contamination must be stopped."

"In the cafeteria?" Angela asked.

"No, no. Although it's bad enough, with all the unnatural additives. But it's the soil I'm concerned about."

"There's dirt in the food?"

"No. Of course not. Someone is contaminating the soil. They've dumped toxic waste. I can feel it. I can hear the cry of the earth—the soil, the tender blades of grass, the harmless plants."

"Nutty," Mrs. Ash said, "what are you talking about?"

Orlando was up again. "He's a little mixed up today," he said. "He's just not himself. Maybe I'd better take him home."

"Are you sick, Nutty?" Mrs. Ash said. She got up and walked toward the front of the room.

"No, I feel wonderful. I have never felt so

relaxed in my whole life. But I've never felt such pain either. I've never thought enough about the agony our planet goes through as we do it such damage. We've got to stop it somehow."

"See what I mean," Orlando said. "I think he's got a touch of temporary insanity. I'll take care of him. He'll be all right by tomorrow."

"The problem is," Nutty said, in a distant voice, as though he were thinking out loud more than talking to anyone, "that we have lost touch. We were once a part of the planet, joined in consciousness, but we have split off, and we don't listen to the music of the universe, the harmony that plays through every living thing."

Orlando suddenly grabbed Nutty and gave him a violent shake. "Nutty, Nutty. Don't do this. You're here. Remember? Student Council. Just be a big jerk, as usual." Bong. Orlando gave him a solid bop on the top of his head.

Nutty felt the shock of reentry and for a moment wanted to go back into the cocoon, the way a waking person resists and drifts back to sleep.

"Nutty. Look at me. Stay with me." But Nutty could feel himself struggling to keep in touch. "Nutty, I'm going to have to take another shot at those stupid things." Suddenly he gave the side of Nutty's head a terrific shot with his open palm, and yelled, "You're a bunch of pigs. You're nothing but mucous and scabs."

Mrs. Ash grabbed Orlando's arm. "Stop that," she said. "What in the world are you doing? Leave him alone."

"I'm not talking to Nutty. It's the little things he's got on his head."

"I don't see any scabs."

But Nutty was shaking his head now. He was back, and scared. He was trying to remember what he had been doing the last little while. "I'm sorry. I . . . I'm sort of mixed up. What were we doing?" And then he whispered to Orlando, "Keep your mouth shut about the photons, will you?"

"Nutty, I'm getting the nurse, if she's still here."

"No, I'm okay. I can manage." And then he looked to the door and saw that William was standing there.

"Mrs. Ash, he's all right," William said. "I know all about this. It's nothing serious at all. I'll take him to his parents."

"Yes. Would you do that?"

William said, "Yes, yes. Just let me manage this. You have no reason to worry." William walked over to Nutty and patted him on the shoulder. "Don't worry. Everything's all right," he whispered.

"Nutty, are you sure you're well enough to walk?" Mrs. Ash asked. "Will you go directly home?"

"Yes. I'm okay now." But he whispered to William, "Those stupid little photons are trying to take over my head."

"I know. I've been listening outside. Isn't it exciting?"

People were filing out of the room now, most of them looking at Nutty, and seeming quite confused. And then one of them switched off the light.

About two seconds passed before William and Orlando seemed to realize the same thing at the same moment—and reacted in the same way. They each grabbed a shoulder and shoved Nutty to his knees, and then they pushed his head under the teacher's desk nearby.

Mrs. Ash was stunned. "Boys. What in the world are you doing?"

Both boys waited for each other for a moment, and then William said, "He needs to get his head down low for a minute—just to clear it, you know. We learn that kind of thing in Boy Scouts."

"Well, don't be so rough about it."

"Oh, that's the whole idea. The sudden movement is what makes the method work."

Mrs. Ash hesitated, as though she were doubtful, but then she called, "Nutty, are you feeling better now?"

"Oh, yeah. I just got a little light-headed there for a second."

"William," Nutty said, "you've got to do something. I think I'm going nuts."

"Nutty, the photons are talking to you. They must be. It's almost too good for me to believe." He had Nutty by the arm and was directing him down the hallway.

"That's what you think. I'm turning into a basket case. I'm acting like those freaks in white robes who wander around warning people that the world is coming to an end."

"No, not at all. You've become concerned about our planet. That's all. The photons are obviously aligned with your brain waves and you feel and understand the harmony in the universe—

things you never have sensed before. It's terrific."

Nutty stopped just before the boys reached the front doors to the school. He turned toward William. "No, William, it's not terrific. It's scary. You have to figure some way to get rid of those things, and you have to do it before it's too late. Another day of this and I don't know if I'll be able to come back. I get floating around in that gold light, and I like it."

"Listen, Nutty, I understand what you're saying. Later on we'll figure out some way to get the photons to leave. But right now we have to take advantage of our opportunity. We have to find out whether the inner world wants to tell us something." He reached up and put a hand on each of Nutty's shoulders, and looked him right in the face. "Look at it this way. The light has chosen you. Your name could very well go down in history as the first person to make contact with inner space."

"Right. Nutty Nutsell—the boy who fell in love with a sandbox. What a moment in history."

"No. Frederick Nutsell, the boy who learned the secrets of the universe—the boy who knows all. All you have to do is listen and tell me what you are learning. I'll try to understand and interpret."

Nutty was scared, and yet William made it sound sort of exciting. Besides, all day he had felt such peace and comfort. There couldn't be anything too wrong with that.

"Come with me, Nutty. Let's use this time."

Nutty wasn't sure what he wanted to do, but he let William pull him along. And when William asked him to lie down on the grass out front, in a nice sunny spot, he was willing to do that. "But William, if I drift off, you'll pull me back, won't you? You won't let me end up in never-never land crying for the weeping willow trees?"

"I promise. Let's just learn what we can—just for a few days, and then we'll get working on sending the photons back to the black box."

"Not a few days, William. Just a few minutes. I don't want to stay in that dream world very long."

"Okay, not long at a stretch. But maybe we can take you in and out several times."

"I'm not sure. Let's try it once; that's all I'll promise for now."

He shut his eyes, let himself feel the warm sun on his body, the gentle grass under his back, the little breeze that touched his face. He was soon drifting, drifting, feeling the wondrous comfort. He seemed to feel the busy buzz of the inner universe, all the perfect action of atomic particles vibrating through him and beyond him, as though there were no end to him, no beginning of grass and soil and air.

"Nutty, can you hear me?"

"Yes."

"Are you seeing the glow that you've talked about?"

"Yes." Nutty opened his eyes, but he saw things through the golden haze. William had crouched next to Nutty and was leaning over him.

"Are the photons saying anything to you?"

"No words."

"But is there something you know—something you are learning?" William had gotten out a little notepad and was holding his pen ready.

"I know there is one universe. There is no separation. No one thing is any more important than any other thing."

"Uh . . . well, I'll have to give that some thought. But are you getting any thoughts that are a little more basic about the way particles function?"

Nutty looked deep within himself. "Matter doesn't matter," he finally said.

"Excuse me?"

"Don't trouble yourself with *things.* "

"But I'm interested to know how things work."

"William, photons do what they do; it's the only thing they can do. They can't do what they don't do."

William hesitated, seemed to consider that. "I'm sorry, Nutty, but that doesn't really clear anything up. It just—" Nutty had begun to speak in a deep and distant voice, like a Gypsy fortune-teller. "Photons know rightness. They do what they do. That is the whole truth. They never do what they can't do, because they don't do what they don't do, and they must do what they do do."

"Look, Nutty, no offense, but all this do-do you're giving me is pretty general. I need something specific I can pass on to the scientists—something about the forces that make things work."

"I will search within myself." He lay very still. He was staring into the sky, but seeing nothing. "Ask a tree how it knows how to grow. Ask a river how it learns to flow. Ask a—"

"Come on, Nutty. What is this—song lyrics? You can do better than that."

Nutty was silent for quite some time, and then he spoke in a slow, soft voice again. "I can only say this. Your mind is limited by the three simple dimensions you know."

William blew out his breath, sounding rather impatient, but then he tried again. "Look, Nutty, that's probably true. But you have to give me something I can understand—with my *limited* mind." William still had his notebook in hand, but he sat back, seemingly less expectant than before. "So, could you just try to avoid the fortune cookie kind of stuff and give me something scientific?"

Nutty lay still for a time again, and when he spoke, it was a sort of chant. "A rock does not fly, but it could. Make a paper airplane and the fibers know 'birdness.' Learn to soar, and you are an eagle, a magpie or a goose. They all soar. Photons soar for the soaring. That is the whole secret."

William was making notes very fast, but when Nutty fell silent again, William looked back, quickly, at what he had written. "Nutty, your material is going downhill, for crying out loud. What's all that gibberish supposed to mean?"

Suddenly Nutty grimaced. "Oh, William, don't speak to me that way. It hurts me so."

"Hey, look, I'm sorry. I didn't mean to—"

"Why must we make pain? Why must we make toxins for the earth and . . . oh, the toxins. They're seeping into things, breaking apart essences, ripping at the core of things. Oh, the pain of it, the awful pain of it." Nutty rolled on his side and pulled his knees up, as though he had a stomachache. "It hurts us so," he moaned. "It's more than we can stand."

"Hey, what's going on? What are you doing to him, William?" Orlando had come out of the school building and had come close to Nutty and William without Nutty noticing. "What do you think you're doing?"

"Be still. He's trying to tell me something. You wouldn't understand."

"Yes, I do. I know about those little fortran things, and I know you're the guy who got them hooked to his head."

William looked up, his arm still resting on Nutty's shoulder. "He shouldn't have shown you that. I plan to make the announcement, but not until I'm ready. You keep quiet about it. Do you hear me?" He pointed a finger at Orlando.

"Hey, don't threaten me. I'll call the cops on you. I think you've let this thing get carried away. Look what you've done to Nutty."

"He's all right." Nutty continued to moan, although more peacefully now, the physical pain having calmed somewhat.

"Oh, sure. Listen to him." Suddenly Orlando knelt down and grabbed Nutty by the shoulder. "Nutty. Nutty. Wake up. You're okay. Wake up."

"Is that my dear friend Orlando?" Nutty said, but still from a distance.

"Leave him alone." William grabbed Orlando's arm and tried to push it away from Nutty's shoulder. "I'm not finished yet."

"Nutty," Orlando yelled. He reached past William with one hand and grabbed Nutty's shirt. "Nutty, wake up. You're here. You're at the school. Come back. Nutty." He and William were struggling all the while, but Orlando had managed to get a good hold on Nutty's shirt and give him a hard shake.

"What? What?" Nutty knew it was Orlando calling to him, but he was confused at the same time. "Orlando?"

"Yeah. It's me. Come back, Nutty. William's trying to mess you up." He dove past William right onto Nutty's chest. He grabbed Nutty up in his arms and rolled away from William. "Nutty, wake up. Everything is all right. The toxins won't hurt you. Nutty, wake up."

William didn't try to interfere this time. In a moment Nutty was shaking his head and looking about. Orlando pulled him to his feet. "Come on," he said. "Come with me. We've got to get you straightened out before William gets you stuck in this dream thing."

"I'm all right," Nutty said. "You shouldn't pull me back so fast. It hurts."

"You were hurting before. You were groaning like you were in a lot of pain."

"It's not a bad hurt. It's all right." Nutty felt himself clinging to the other consciousness.

"Nutty," William said, "I'm sorry. I was trying to understand. But it all sounded like a bunch of gobbledygook. I think you're going to have to practice interpreting what you're seeing."

"I know," Nutty said. "I guess what I said was weird, but it all made sense to me at the time."

"No, it didn't," Orlando said. He pulled on Nutty's shoulder, twisting him around. "You're weird when you're like that. You're loony-tunes, Nutty. You shouldn't mess with it."

And that seemed true too. Nutty was coming further away from the glow with every second, and the fear was setting back in.

"Nutty, come with me," William said. He got up and took hold of Nutty's arm.

But Orlando grabbed the other one tighter. "No, Nutty. Stay away from him. Come with me. William's going to mess you up."

"Nutty," William said, "it's so important that we probe this thing. I really don't think there's any danger."

"Let go," Nutty said to both of them. "Just let me go. I have to think."

He pulled both arms loose. He wanted to get closer to the big sycamore tree not far away, wanted to get hold of it, embrace it. But something told him that hugging a sycamore was definitely a strange thing to do.

10

Nutty decided to leave. Orlando and William were still waiting nearby, but he told them both he needed some time alone, and he walked home. He slipped quietly into his room, pulled the curtains closed, and lay on his bed, leaving the light off. He wanted to try something he had been thinking about on the way home. He wanted to feel some of the glow, but not lose contact with his room and all the real things around him. He wondered if he could have both ways of seeing and feeling at the same time.

He lay on his bed in the dim light, felt himself drift into harmony with the photons, and yet he fought to see the dimly lighted room—the chair near his bed, his baseball glove lying on his desk, the posters on the wall . . .

And then his bedroom door opened.

A second or two passed before Nutty realized that his mother was standing there, looking at him. And another second passed before he could react. He twisted and rolled, slipped down to the floor, and stuck his head under the bed.

"Freddie," his mom gasped. "What's wrong?"

"Nothing. I'm just looking for something."

"But what's wrong with your head?"

"Nothing. What are you talking about? Could you flip the light on, Mom?" When he heard the click of the light switch, he pulled his head out from under the bed, and looked up, hesitantly. "I guess it's not down there."

"What?"

"What I was looking for."

"Freddie, your head was . . . glowing in the dark."

Nutty laughed, trying not to sound nervous. He leaned back against his bed, still sitting on the floor. "How could my head glow?"

"I don't know. You tell me."

"It must have been an optical illusion or something, I guess."

But Mom was studying Nutty closely. He knew

she was more than a little suspicious. "The room was dark, but I could see your face. There was a glow all the way around your head."

Nutty forced himself to laugh again. "Oh, that. It must have been my flashlight. I was reading in the dark."

"Freddie, you don't have a book."

"Oh, yeah . . . I know. That's what I was looking for under my bed."

"Where's the flashlight?"

"It must be down there too."

"Freddie, I want to know what's going on. You weren't reading; you were just lying there—and your face was all lit up."

"Oh, yeah . . . now I think I know what you're talking about. I ran all the way home, and I was resting—and then I was going to read—with my flashlight—which might be under my bed—but I couldn't find it—and I was probably all red in the face from running."

"Freddie, that's absolute nonsense." She flipped the light back off and Nutty made another dive under the bed. "Son, you come out of there and tell me what's going on."

"Just a minute. Would you turn the light on so I can see under here?"

"No. You come out so I can look at you."

Nutty was in a panic. He felt around for anything he could get his hands on. His hand struck his baseball cap and he grabbed it and put it on. And then he found something else—a piece of cloth of some sort. He wrapped that around his face and around his neck, and then he slid out and peeked up. "Now see, I don't glow in the dark."

"What have you got on your—"

She flipped the light on again and Nutty took another dive.

"Freddie, what in the world are you doing?"

"Trying to find my flashlight. Oh, yeah, and here it is." Nutty crawled backward, flipped the flashlight on, then sat up and directed the light on his face. "Did I look sort of like this?"

"No. Not at all."

"Well, then, I guess it wasn't my flashlight. That at least clears that up."

"Freddie, nothing is cleared up. Why did you just wrap a pair of your shorts around your face, if you're not hiding something?"

"My shorts? Was that my shorts? Oh, sick."

Mom was getting mad; Nutty could see that. She was leaning against the wall, and she had folded her arms. Her lips were pressed tight, the way they got when she had taken all she was going to take. "Freddie, you tell me what's going on, and tell me right now."

"Nothing to worry about, Mom. Really."

"Then what are you trying to hide?"

"Can you trust me to tell you in a few days? It's

something sort of secret, and something to do with my science-fair project, and something to do with William, and sort of a surprise."

"Is something wrong with your head?"

"No. Not at all."

"Wasn't it glowing?"

"No, no. It might look that way. But it was really some light shining on my head. A guy's head can't glow." And that was the truth, Nutty told himself. Light was around his head; it wasn't coming *from* his head.

Mom was still looking worried—and suspicious. "Freddie, you were acting very strange this morning. And you're acting strange now."

"Dad says I always act strange. What else is new?"

"This is a new kind of strange."

"Yeah, well—that's progress, I guess. A guy can't rely on his old material forever."

"Freddie, I have the feeling that you're nervous, that you're trying to cover up something. That worries me. Why don't you just tell me what you and William have been up to?"

"It's just a science project. You know William. He always thinks up something good. You'll have to come over to school and see our display on Saturday—then you'll understand all about it. It's just a little experiment with light and that sort of thing." Nutty was thinking that maybe he ought to come clean and explain the whole thing, including the strange effect the photons were having on him. But he knew she would worry herself sick. Once the photons were gone, he could tell her all about it, and she wouldn't get so upset. He was glad when the phone rang and she left the room to answer it.

As it turned out, William was on the phone. He didn't admit it, but he seemed worried. At first Nutty thought he was only upset because Nutty had made so little sense, but gradually it became clear that he was wondering whether Nutty was going off the deep end. This was anything but comforting, and besides, Nutty could say very little with his mother in the room. Finally, they just agreed to meet the next day, and William gave Nutty a long speech about keeping things under control. "Pinch yourself, or whatever you have to do, but don't get too deep into this thing at school tomorrow. After school, let's see if we can get something better out of you, and then we might have to try to get rid of the photons. We don't want you to go crackers on us."

"Thanks a lot, William. You've been a big help."

"Yes, well, I don't mean to alarm you. But you'll have to admit, you were saying some weird things this afternoon."

Nutty tried to think back. It had all made such good sense then, and it seemed so stupid now.

"Yeah, well," he finally said, "they're *your* photons." He said good-bye and hung up the phone.

"What's a photon?" his mother said. She was still watching him very carefully.

"It's a little hunk of light."

"Is that what your experiment is about?"

"Exactly. Now we've got the whole thing cleared up." He walked out of the kitchen, and his mother let him go. But he glanced back and saw that her lips were still tight. She was going to be watching him closely now, and he was going to have to watch himself around her.

Nutty felt strange all evening. His homework came easily to him and he was done in half the usual time, but he kept having to knock himself in the head to keep from drifting entirely out of himself.

When he awoke in the morning, the process was as natural as the opening of a flower. He flowed through the morning. He felt things intensely, seemed to see and hear everything more vividly than ever before, noticed the pungent smell and taste of the very air around him.

He read with such concentration that morning that the pages became reality, his mind conjuring the images so sharply that he seemed transported to the fictional world. And when he looked up, he found joy in the things around him: the gracious chalk that gave up its existence, bit by bit, as it was scraped across the board, and all for the sake of the students; the fine window glass that had accepted the torture of heat and stress, all to clarify itself, to grant the vision of the great outdoors; the fantastic array of colors and tints in every existing "thing" in the room. The world was so amazing to look at, to breathe in, to taste and smell and touch. Why had he never really sensed it all before?

When Mrs. Smiley told the students they could go outside, Nutty rose from his desk and hurried out to the trees and grass, the rocks and gravel. He was overwhelmed with thankfulness that his school allowed him a recess. He breathed in the cool air, drank in the aroma of the blossoming trees.

He was taking his fourth or fifth deep breath when Sarah stopped in front of him. "Nutty, what are you doing?"

Nutty spoke in a calm, deep voice. "I caught a whiff of the blossoms in these lovely little crab apple trees. The smell is so sweet it makes my head swim. Breathe some of it in, Sarah; it will add such joy to your morning."

"Nutty, lay off. You're not as funny as you think you are." But her voice lacked conviction. She seemed to know that Nutty was actually serious.

"What do you mean, Sarah?"

"Nutty, what's with you? I think you're cracking up."

"It's the photons, Sarah. I'm surrounded with photons, millions of little particles, filling my head with such a sense of the connectedness of the universe that I want to cry with joy."

"Nutty, don't talk so loud. You're acting like the world's biggest wimp. People are going to laugh you right out of school."

"No, no. I love everyone too much. They must know that."

Sarah looked around, as though she were afraid someone might hear. "Look, Nutty, I don't know what you're doing. But it's stupid, and it's weird. Maybe you think it's funny, or maybe you're trying to take on some whole new image because everyone teased you about being dumb, but—"

"No, Sarah. It's nothing like that. I've changed, and for the better. I never want to be like that silly kid I used to be. I want to be—"

"Nutty, shut up. You can't go around talking about love and blossoms and stuff like that. If you tell people you love them, they're going to—"

"But I do, Sarah. I love you." He suddenly reached out and wrapped his arms around her. "Oh, I love you so much. You're one of the dearest persons I've ever known."

Sarah had been taken by surprise, but she quickly struggled to get away, and when she did, she looked all around to see who was watching. A group of her friends had been waiting, not far away, and they were going crazy, laughing as though they would lose their minds.

"Nutty, you're nuts," Sarah said. "Don't ever do that again."

"I'm sorry," Nutty said. "I only meant to tell you how much I cared for—"

But suddenly a hand clamped over his mouth, and Nutty heard Orlando's voice in his ear. "Nutty, stop it. Don't say another word. We gotta get you straightened out before they take you away in a straitjacket."

Nutty heard the urgency in Orlando's voice, but he had to laugh. Poor Orlando didn't understand.

"I'm going to take my hand off your mouth, but don't start any of that love stuff again."

Nutty waited a moment, stepped away from Orlando, and then said, "But I do love her, Orlando. And I love you even more."

Thud. Orlando blasted Nutty with both hands, right in the chest. Nutty stumbled backward and landed flat on his fanny. And at the same moment the lovely calm lifted from his mind. "Hey, watch it!" he said. "You wanna get your block knocked off?"

"All right. Now that's what I wanted to hear," Orlando said. "I think I just knocked those pontoon things right out of existence."

"Photons," Nutty said, but he was trying to decide whether Orlando really had scared them off. He was waiting for their gentleness.

"Are they gone?"

"I don't know. Maybe."

"Let's see." Orlando grabbed Nutty's jacket and jerked it up over his head, and then closed it around his face as tight as he could.

"Hey, be careful. Are you trying to pull my head off?"

Orlando parted the jacket just a little and looked in at Nutty's face. "Oh, man," he said. "Those stupid things just don't know when to take off."

"Am I still glowing?"

"Yes."

"What about my left ear? Did you cut it all the way off with the zipper, or just halfway?" Orlando let the jacket go and Nutty pulled it away from his face and back into some semblance of order. "I think I'll cut about three of *your* ears off. That hurt."

"You ought to thank me. I just kept you from turning into a permanent idiot."

"Yeah, well, thanks. I wouldn't want to be in your condition all my life."

"Geez, Nutty, you're either trying to hug me or you're acting like a jerk. Can't you find something in between?"

Nutty didn't answer, but he was wondering the same thing. And the truth was, he was sort of scared.

11

The boys stayed away from the other kids during the rest of the recess time, and they talked about what they ought to do. "Nutty, listen to me," Orlando said. "This afternoon let's go over to my house and try to find some way to get rid of those things. Maybe we can squirt your head with a hose or something like that."

"I don't know, Orlando. William is going to try to get rid of them, but he still wants to see if we can't learn something first."

"Oh, sure. That's fine for William. But he doesn't see you over here turning into a cream-filled Twinkie."

"Hey, I'm not. I just—"

"Nutty, you're going around telling people you love them—even girls, for crying out loud. You're raving about the pain shrubs are feeling."

Nutty was trying to remember what he had meant. "I just care—or at least I cared—about Sarah and . . . about everything. I felt really good when I was saying all that."

"It's stupid, Nutty. It's embarrassing. You'd realize that if those python things would leave you alone."

"That's a snake, stupid."

"Well, maybe that's what those things are," Orlando said. "They're crawling into your brain. You're the only guy I know who thinks he's Tinker Bell half the time and Godzilla the rest. We've got to do something. Let's think. What could we do to terrorize those things?"

Nutty didn't answer. He could feel himself beginning to relax, to let himself accept the gentle, soft touch of the—Blaaaaahhhhh! Nutty flinched and then jumped back. "Orlando, what the heck?"

Orlando had sprung at Nutty, screaming and making an awful face. He had certainly scared Nutty, whether or not he had alarmed the photons.

"We've gotta let 'em know we don't want 'em," Orlando said. He suddenly started making chopping motions at Nutty's head.

"Watch it," Nutty said.

But Orlando was making wild swings at Nutty,

like a stuntman in a movie, always missing, but making the gestures look as real as possible. Nutty was flinching and dodging. "I'm not going to let those things make you crazy. We've got to try everything we can think of."

Nutty dodged another karate chop, and then jumped back a little farther. "Stop it, will you? You're the one who's going nuts."

"You're back with me again, aren't you? At least doing this keeps you around, even if it doesn't scare the pythons away." Suddenly he jumped forward, let out a terrible war cry, and chopped both arms at Nutty's head. Nutty stumbled and fell, and Orlando came down on top of him, but instead of rolling off, he sat on Nutty's chest and threw about ten shots at Nutty's head, never missing by more than an inch. "Get lost, do you hear me? Take off, you stupid little things. We hate you, and we want you to go back where you came from."

Nutty was yelling all the while for Orlando to stop it and to get off. And then, without warning, Orlando went flying. Nutty looked up to see that Bilbo had run over and knocked Orlando for a loop. "What do you think you're doing?" he said.

"Geez, Bilbo," Orlando mumbled, with his face still in the grass, "are you nuts too? You about killed me."

"What are you beating up on Nutty for?"

Orlando rolled over on his back and started to

laugh. "Hey, I wasn't. Really. I was trying to scare away those—"

Richie had come up behind Bilbo now. "Would someone tell me what the heck is going on? Nutty's going around hugging people and kissing trees, and Orlando's acting like a madman, knocking the heck out of his own best friend."

"No, I wasn't. Not really."

"Then what are you doing?"

"I was trying to help Nutty. That's all I'm saying. And if you ever get in trouble, I'll be glad to help you the same way."

Orlando was laughing, but Richie wasn't. "What kind of trouble?"

"Orlando, that's enough." Nutty got up. "Listen, we were just messing around. There's something going on, but I can't explain it yet. I'll tell you about it when I can."

"But one thing," Orlando said. He was sitting up now, but he was still down on the grass. "You can help Nutty. He's gotta make it through this day without turning weird on us again."

"Orlando, don't—"

"I don't care, Nutty. We've got to get you through this." He got up and walked over to Bilbo and Richie. "Every chance you get today, try to surprise Nutty. Slug him on the shoulder or make a noise in his ear. And if he starts looking like his eyes are going blank, shove him out of his desk or something. Mrs. Smiley might get mad, but if we don't help Nutty, he's going to be Tinker Bell forever."

Nutty assured the boys that Orlando was wrong and that they should ignore him entirely. But as recess ended, and the boys headed back to class, Nutty saw Orlando pull Bilbo and Richie aside and have a quick but intense conversation with them.

Between recess and lunch the chaos began. Nutty was fighting to keep himself in touch with what was going on around him, but about the time he felt himself drifting away, he was startled back to reality. Orlando walked by him, dropped a dictionary, picked it up, dropped it again, reached for it, stumbled and fell on his face. As he got up, he fell against Nutty's shoulder and shoved an elbow into his neck.

The kids in the class all laughed, and Mrs. Smiley was skeptical that the whole thing was an accident. "Orlando," she said, "please go to your seat. That's about enough of that. What are you doing over there anyway?"

Orlando was leaning over Nutty. "Are you with the living?" he said.

"Of course. Lay off." But Nutty knew he had been pulled back.

All the same, the barrage continued. Nutty got hit by a spitwad in the side of the head, and then a piece of chalk missed by inches, whizzed past his nose and broke against the wall. Mrs. Smiley heard the noise and looked up, but she wasn't sure what had happened. Nutty looked over at Orlando and shook his head, but soon after that he got a note, passed from the girl between him and Orlando. The note said:

Nutty,
"Fight the pithons don't let them get you. Stick the point of this compass (rapped up in this paper) in your leg or arm if you have to but not to deep.

Your best friend,
Orlando

Nutty was not about to stick a sharp object in his leg, but he had to admit he was drifting a little again when Orlando, Bilbo, and Richie were all seized with a coughing fit at the same time. Mrs. Smiley chided them for that too, but Orlando sounded as though he were breaking in half before he let up and asked to go get a drink. And returning, he took the long way, past Nutty's desk, and somehow acquired a whole new way of walking, with hips swinging so wildly that he bumped Nutty halfway out of his desk.

It was a good thing that lunch came soon after that, because Mrs. Smiley had had just about enough. She gave a very stern warning that no such nonsense would continue after lunch. Orlando promised, but while the boys were eating, he put

Nutty on notice that he might have to get by without help, and that he'd better use the compass in the leg—or in the ear—if that's what it took. Nutty was hardly paying attention, and Orlando had to elbow him three or four times to get him through lunch.

Nutty fought the good battle, but he felt like a person trying to keep from falling asleep after not getting any rest for days. He had no sooner gotten back to class than he let go, drifted into the tender arms of golden loveliness, felt all the rightness and comfort pump into him.

Mrs. Smiley was talking—about the geography and climate of New Zealand—and pointing to a map. Nutty was thinking of the people there.

"Nutty, are you listening to me?"

Nutty heard Mrs. Smiley, and he was moved by her concern for him, her obvious desire to reach all her students. "Oh, yes, Mrs. Smiley. Thank you for this fascinating information."

"Nutty, stop that. I don't think you were listening, and I'm tired of all the showing off you've been doing."

"Oh, but I *was* listening, and I was thinking about all those lovely people in New Zealand— especially the good Maori people. Their culture is certainly fascinating."

A lot of the kids started to laugh, and Orlando dropped his dictionary again.

"Nutty, that's enough of that. Do you hear me?

And Orlando, if you drop one more book, you're going to the office. I'm very upset with both of you. I think you've decided to put on this little farce because it gets a few laughs, but it is interrupting class, and I won't have it."

"Don't be mad at us," Nutty said, in a soft, kindly voice. "Orlando is worried about me, and he's trying to help me. He's doing things he shouldn't, but he means well. And I know I seem changed, but I'm all right. I've never felt more whole and complete in my life."

"But you look like you've fallen to pieces, Nutty dear," Mindy said, in a falsetto voice. Everyone laughed.

"But Mrs. Smiley, I'm completely serious," Nutty continued. "I'm filled with appreciation now for every person and thing on earth—all the plants, all the trees, the lovely flowers that grace our planet with color and aroma. I feel as if I'm one with the soil—the good clean dirt that collects under my fingernails when I work—the sand in my shoes when I return from a hike, the smell of—"

"Your dirty socks." This was from Mindy again. Most of the kids laughed, but rather nervously. They seemed to have sensed Nutty's seriousness, and they were watching him, obviously wondering what was going on.

"Oh, Mindy, why try to hurt me by saying something so unkind?" Nutty asked. He stood up and reached out a hand toward her. He wanted to touch her and soften the feelings between them.

"I'll tell you what. I'll hug Mindy, just to show her how much I—ugh!"

Nutty was suddenly knocked backward. He landed in a sitting position on his desk. Orlando's dictionary, which up until then had only had problems with falling, had taken to flying. It caught Nutty right in the chest.

Nutty grabbed his chest, fought for breath, and at the same time felt his head clear. But suddenly he was outraged. "Orlando, you idiot," he yelled. "Are you trying to kill me?" He jumped from his seat and dove across the desk between them. He grabbed for Orlando's neck, but Orlando fell back in terror, and Nutty missed him. "You'd *better* stay out of my reach," Nutty yelled. "I'll break you in half if I get hold of you."

12

Nutty and Orlando were standing in the hallway, facing Mrs. Smiley, and she was saying that she was shocked at their behavior. Nutty was really embarrassed that he had lost his temper, and he was vaguely aware that a few minutes before his behavior had been even more unusual. He had offered to hug Mindy? Sick!

"My goodness, Orlando. I can't believe you threw that huge dictionary at your best friend. And Nutty, what in the world is wrong with you today?"

"Mrs. Smiley," Orlando said, "there actually is a reason for all this stuff. Nutty does have something wrong with him. He can't help what he's been doing."

"Is that true, Nutty? Is something wrong?"

Nutty was looking at the floor. He felt like the world's biggest jerk. "I'm okay now."

"Would you like to explain to me what's going on?"

"It's William Bilks's fault," Orlando said. "He got Nutty involved in an experiment, and now—"

"I'm okay now, Orlando. You don't have to go into all that."

"I know what I ought to do," Mrs. Smiley said. "I ought to march both of you to the principal's office. But I really hate to do that. You're both very nice young men most of the time."

"Mrs. Smiley, Orlando wasn't trying to hurt me with that dictionary. He was trying to . . . help me. But I can't explain any more than that."

Mrs. Smiley looked anything but satisfied, but she said, "Well, I'm willing to give both of you another chance. But we'll have no more of this kind of foolishness. Is that understood?"

Both boys nodded, and then all three walked back into class. The kids were staring at Nutty, but Nutty slipped into his seat and tried to avoid everyone's eyes. Mindy turned around and said, "You'd better keep your hands off me, Nutty. If you try to hug me again, I'll—"

"Look, Mindy, I'd rather kiss a slug than touch you, so don't worry about it, all right?"

Mrs. Smiley began to talk about New Zealand

again. Nutty tried really hard to listen. But he was preoccupied. He kept wondering whether he would ever be normal again. He could just imagine what the other kids—especially Sarah—must be thinking about him.

But before long Nutty was drifting again. He heard the faint sound of the breeze in the little crab apple tree out in front, picked up the smell of a lawn being mowed somewhere on campus, and he thought he heard the soil busily drinking up water from the gentle sprinklers in front of the building. He thought of the slugs. Why had he insulted those sleek, pretty creatures, who were only playing their part in the great scheme of the universe?

Mrs. Smiley said she now was going to show a film about New Zealand, and Nutty sat back and relaxed, waiting for the film to start.

"Would someone turn out the lights?" The film started at almost the same instant. The first green vision of New Zealand was breathtaking.

And then Nutty was attacked.

Someone was struggling with him, pulling at the collar of his shirt. "Pull your shirt over your head. Hurry. Help me." By instinct, Nutty struggled to get free, even after he realized that it was Orlando who was tugging at his T-shirt. "Your head, Nutty. Cover up your head."

Nutty was suddenly clear about what was happening, and terrified at the idea that everyone would see him glowing in the dark. He grabbed the neck of his shirt and pulled his head down inside, like a scared turtle. All the while, he could hear Mrs. Smiley saying, "Orlando, whatever are you doing? Someone turn the lights on."

Nutty could tell when the light came on. He quickly pulled at his shirt and let his head pop out. He looked around to see that everyone was staring at him again, looking shocked, baffled.

"Orlando, you promised me to stop this kind of behavior. And the first thing you do is start another fight. Now both of you report to Dr. Dunlop's office this minute."

"I wasn't fighting with him. I was . . . trying to help him . . . again."

"Orlando, that's enough nonsense. If you help him any more, you'll have him in the hospital. Both of you leave right now. I'll be down to the office in just a minute."

"Mrs. Smiley," someone said, "Nutty's head looked funny. I thought he was a ghost there for a minute."

"What?"

Nutty was staring at his desk. This was awful.

"He looked like one of those Christmas decorations that has a light bulb inside and a Santa Claus face."

Nutty took a peek at Mrs. Smiley, who was anything but smiley at the moment. "Christmas decoration?"

"I saw something too," someone else said. "I thought he had a flashlight on his face."

"No, it was more like a glow."

Mrs. Smiley stopped in front of him, and touched the back of her hand to his forehead. "Do you feel okay? You don't have a fever," she said.

"Honest, Mrs. Smiley," Orlando said, "we weren't fighting. Something is bothering Nutty, and I was trying to help him. I think I'd better take him to the nurse, or maybe even home."

Mrs. Smiley looked more confused than angry now, but she said, "Orlando, sit down. Nutty can walk just fine. I want him to go to the nurse. But don't think you two are off the hook. We may be paying a visit to Dr. Dunlop yet."

Nutty got up and thanked Mrs. Smiley. He was too embarrassed to look at anyone else. He walked out the door calmly, but then he hurried down the hallway. He went past the office and the nurse's station, and kept going right on out the front doors. The only person who might be able to help him was William, who wouldn't be home yet, but at least Nutty knew he had to get away from everyone else.

Nutty walked down the street, shaking his head, and then when he feared he was drifting again, he began slapping himself in the face. At one point, a woman working in her yard looked up from her flowers and saw Nutty slug himself in the forehead. She looked rather stunned, but Nutty hurried on. By the time he got to William's place, he was pinching his arm and stopping to stomp on his own toes—anything to keep himself out of the haze.

But then he made a mistake. He went to William's backyard. He knew he would have to wait quite some time, and so he sat down and leaned against a tree. A minute later the photons took over and he felt united with a limb of the tree. He sensed a gentle swaying to the movement of the air, the firm pull of gravity, the nice hold of the dear old tree trunk, felt the subtle joy of the leaves as they photosynthesized, drinking in the good sun, filling up his soul with chlorophyll.

Time passed in this perfect state—hours—but Nutty was beyond time. Slowly he became less limb, more earth and water and air. He knew he was part of the universe, pulsing, slowly turning, interconnected.

"Nutty! Nutty!" Something slapped him across the face.

Nutty started, and then jumped to his feet. "William, don't do that. You scared me half to death."

"You were in a coma or something. I spoke to you five times. I had no choice but to slap you."

Nutty was breathing hard. "Look, William, you've got to help me." He looked at his watch. "My gosh. I've been a tree limb for about three hours."

"You've been out here all afternoon?"

Nutty had a hard time remembering for a moment, and then the whole thing at school came back to him. He sat down on the grass and grabbed his head in his hands. "Yeah. I got talking really weird in Mrs. Smiley's class. And then we had a film. They turned the light out and I lit up. Mrs. Smiley sent me to the school nurse."

"What did the nurse say?"

"Nothing. I skipped her and came looking for you. I need to find a way out of this mess before I turn into a tulip or a daffodil or something."

"Well, you'll be in trouble at school. We'll have to do what we can about that. Maybe we'd better try to get rid of the photons now . . . if we can."

"Yeah, I think so. What do we have to do?"

"Well . . . I'm not sure. I have a couple of ideas."

Nutty lay back and covered his face with his hands. "Don't do this to me, William. You've gotta have something better than a couple of ideas."

"Hey, my theories worked to *attract* the photons. I don't see why they won't work to send them away."

Nutty sat up. "Look, don't convince *me.* Convince *them.*"

"Okay. But let me explain what I'm thinking. We attracted the photons by making them feel compatible with you—or with your brain. Right?"

"I guess so."

"Okay. What we have to do is get all the waves out of sync again. We need to introduce a hostile environment."

"William, you gotta be kidding. Is that all you can think of? Orlando and I have been trying that for two days."

"Really?"

"Oh, brother." Nutty dropped on his back on the grass again. Now he knew he was in trouble. "William, we've called those little suckers every name in the book. We've karate chopped 'em, slapped 'em—you name it—and they don't scare off."

"Ah, well, I have something more sophisticated than that in mind."

"Well, what is it?" Nutty got up. "Do I get back in the box?"

"Maybe." William stood up too. But he leaned against the tree, and Nutty could see that he was going into one of his deep thought sessions. A couple of minutes went by before he said, "I can think of two things that the photons may not be able to tolerate."

"Okay. What are they? Let's go try them both—at the same time." Nutty took a couple of steps toward the house.

"Wait. Just a minute. Let me explain what I'm thinking. Sit down here again. We need to talk."

William sat down on the grass again, but Nutty didn't. "Just tell me, okay. I want to get on with this."

"All right. As I see it, the photons will not synchronize with your brain if it starts to think of harsh, cruel things."

"No way, William. I grabbed at Orlando this afternoon, and I was ready to break his bones."

"Maybe the photons gave you the benefit of the doubt. Maybe they knew you wouldn't really do it."

"So what does that mean? I have to beat somebody up to get rid of them?"

"Well . . . maybe." William was looking up at Nutty, and Nutty could still see his mind was working. "Maybe you could do something cruel to some*thing* instead of some*one*. You know . . . kill some grass . . . or something like that."

Nutty felt a sudden chill go through him, almost a panic. "Look, William, I don't want to kill grass. There's got to be some better way than that."

"Hey, just a little patch of grass. What could that hurt? It grows back. You could dump some gasoline on it, or—"

"No, I won't do that."

"Wow. That's interesting."

Now they were staring at each other, and they were both realizing the same thing.

"Isn't there some other way?"

"I don't know, Nutty. Maybe you could kill something else. How do you feel about mice?"

Nutty looked within himself for a time. "I think I could kill a mosquito, or a fly . . . but I'd rather not."

"I don't know, Nutty. Even photons probably hate mosquitoes. That may not do it. I think you'd have a lot better shot if you killed your little sister's goldfish."

"William!"

"All right. All right. But do you want out of this thing or don't you?"

"I do. But you'd better think of some other way—noisy music and ugly scenes and no magnets and—"

"Nutty, I've already thought about stuff like that. But you've been in that kind of environment since the beginning and the photons haven't left." William stood up again. He put a hand on Nutty's shoulder. "I just don't think that will work, but we could try it."

"What's going to work then? You said you had a *couple* of ideas."

"Okay. The other one is a totally blank mind. If we could make your mind go blank—not a thought in it—I'm thinking that the photons would lose interest."

"So how do we do that?"

"Maybe through hypnotism—the way we did when you were playing basketball."

"Okay. Let's try it."

William took a deep breath and shoved his hands down in his pockets. He was facing Nutty, but he wasn't looking him in the eye now. "But I was also thinking . . . what if we waited and we did it at the science fair?"

"Science fair? I forgot all about it. When is it?"

"Tomorrow."

"You're kidding. We don't have a project."

"What are you talking about? We've got you lighting up the night. I could get some scientists there—and the press. It could be our big moment. If we got rid of the photons now, no one would ever know what we accomplished."

"William, I can't hold out. If I go to sleep tonight, I'll wake up thinking I'm a lilac bush in the morning. In some ways I like the experience, but it's getting me in trouble. I don't think I can take it anymore."

"Okay. We'll keep you up all night. And we'll do what we have to do to keep you from drifting off too far. Then tomorrow, right in front of everyone, we'll try to chase the photons back to the box. If we can pull that off, we'll be famous before the sun goes down tomorrow night. And if we fail, at least we'll have proof that the photons are with you, and we can try to get the scientists to help reverse what we've done."

"I can't stay up all night."

"Sure you can. You had a nice nap this afternoon. We'll ask your parents if you can stay with me tonight. We'll—"

"My parents. What if someone's called my mom by now?"

"Yes, well, we'll just have to deal with that. I have a feeling we might as well tell your parents what's going on at this point. They'll find out tomorrow anyway."

"They'll go nuts if we tell them I have a light around my head."

"Oh, no. I doubt that. If we explain the whole thing, logically and carefully, I'm sure they'll be understanding and supportive—maybe even excited for us."

13

"A Light Around His Head?!!" Mr. Nutsell came right out of his seat. "What do you mean, there's a light around his head?"

"I'm pretty sure it's not dangerous, sir. And I really don't think it's permanent. I have several ideas about—"

"You don't *think* it's permanent?"

Nutty leaned forward and let his chin rest in his two hands, his elbows on his knees. He had known exactly what to expect, even if William hadn't. Mom was shaking her head. "Fred, don't panic. I'm sure everything will be fine."

"But really," William said, "you need to look on the bright side of all this."

"Right," Dad said. "I certainly want to thank you, William. I see the bright side all right. I'll place my son here in the living room and use him for a floor lamp."

"No, no. I'll have him back to normal by tomorrow." William was pacing now, the way he did when he was about to begin one of his lofty speeches. "Sir, how would you like to have been Newton's father, or closer to home, the father of Ben Franklin or Thomas Edison? What an honor—and what a reflection on you, sir!"

"Freddie's a reflection all right. But Edison invented the electric light; you didn't have to invent the first human one." Mr. Nutsell dropped back into his chair and folded his arms across his chest.

"William, explain the experiment again," Mom said. "I guess I don't understand what it is you are trying to accomplish."

William went into one of his lengthy scientific dissertations. Mrs. Nutsell listened carefully, and seemed quite interested. Mr. Nutsell kept shaking his head and rolling his eyes.

But then something caught Dad's attention. "What's that you say about reporters?"

"I did some calling before we came over here. I talked to reporters from here in town, and in Kansas City. I think we'll have plenty of TV cameras going when we release those photons. I also have two professors scheduled to come—one from the college here, and one from the University of Missouri. They know me, and they trust me; I explained enough to them that they know I'm on to something."

"You mean the reporters believed you that you had some sort of scientific breakthrough?"

"Well, actually, I stressed the idea that Nutty's head glows in the dark. That's the sort of thing that plays well to the media." Nutty cringed. He could just imagine how ridiculous he would look.

"He won't come off looking stupid on the evening news, will he?"

"Stupid? About as stupid as the Wright brothers looked at Kitty Hawk. About as stupid as Neil Armstrong looked stepping onto the moon. I suspect the footage that is shot tomorrow will wind up in the Smithsonian. And you'll want to be there, sir. I'm sure the reporters will want to interview you and find out what you did to produce such a brilliant child."

"Really? Well . . ."

Needless to say, William was very proud of himself. A few minutes later he was sitting backward on Nutty's desk chair, his short little legs wrapped around the chairback. "I told you your dad would be no problem. Logic always wins out in the end—especially if you combine it with cheap flattery." He chuckled to himself. Nutty was lying on his bed, relaxing, glad that his parents had not gotten any angrier than they had.

"I'm a little disappointed your parents insisted we stay here tonight," William said. "But I can get our things together in the morning, I suppose. I'm thinking we ought to experiment a little, maybe try to—Nutty, are you listening?"

Nutty was listening, sort of, way out there somewhere. He thought of answering William, but then, somehow it seemed that William must know his thoughts.

"Nutty! Can you hear me?"

Suddenly, Nutty felt William's knees on his chest and a double slap, one on each cheek.

"Hey, watch it!"

"I'm sorry. I let you slip away. I was too busy talking, and I let you float right out of here."

"I'm okay. Just let me sleep for a while."

"Nutty, you don't want to do that. If you get too far out, we don't know whether you can get back. Remember?"

"I don't think it's a problem. It's just comfortable and peaceful, and so full of . . . beauty . . . and—"

"Nutty, get up. Stand up and walk around." William pulled on Nutty's arm, dragged him off the bed. Nutty put his feet down to avoid crashing to the floor, and then he stood up. "All right now, walk."

"I don't want to."

"Okay, then, take a shower."

"Yeah, that would be nice. Or maybe a bath."

"A shower. Ice cold." William pushed Nutty down on the bed again, and tugged off his shoes and socks. In a few minutes Nutty was yelping with pain, as William turned on the shower—cold water only.

Nutty was certainly back to reality. When Susie came to the bathroom door and asked what was wrong, he told her to mind her own business or he would stick her head in the toilet. "That's good," William said. "Excellent. Now you're sounding like the Nutty we all know and love."

As it turned out, the evening was long, and the night was even longer. Orlando showed up soon after the cold shower, wondering what had happened, and he agreed to stay overnight and help keep Nutty in touch with things—and out of love with any houseplants or wandering spiders.

They fed Nutty; made him do exercises; tried to make him laugh. And when all else failed, they punched him around a little.

By three o'clock, however, William was dealing with Orlando as much as with Nutty. He kept making Orlando walk Nutty around the room, and from time to time he would startle them by suddenly jumping in front of them with bared claws, or by shooting them with Nutty's squirt gun.

By five o'clock William was fighting as much with himself. It was about seven-fifteen when Mrs. Nutsell came into the room and found all three of them sacked out in various places about the room. She almost tripped on Orlando, who was spread across the floor.

"Boys, what are you doing?" she said.

Nutty heard this through a filter of lovely light. But then he felt a crack on the side of the head. "Nutty, Nutty. Come back. Come back."

"Stop it, William. What are you doing?"

"Help me, ma'am," Nutty heard William say. "I need to get him in a cold shower. If he drifts too far out into the universe he may choose not to return."

"What? William, you didn't tell us anything like that last night."

"I know. I know. But help me. I'll get him into the shower; you go turn the air conditioner on."

Nutty sleepwalked his way into the bathroom, and then screamed his way back to his bedroom, naked as the day he was born. "William, I'm going to squash you if you ever do anything like that again."

But William was in the hallway, assuring Nutty's mother that his little nude dash was a very good sign, and anger and hatred were clear evidence that the boy was no longer in the world of the photons.

"You mean they're gone?" she asked.

"I doubt that. They haven't left so far, and we've abused them pretty badly."

"Then what makes you so sure you can get rid of them this afternoon?"

"Well, I never said I was sure; I just said—"

"Oh, William, you're going to be the death of me. What will you think of next?"

"It's hard to say," William said, grinning. "But I can't wait myself. It's usually something good."

Mrs. Nutsell was rolling her eyes, looking much like her husband.

A few hours later, William and Nutty were standing in the school gymnasium among the science-fair displays, and in front of their own black box. All the news media was ready, but William was looking less thrilled with his own wit, and Nutty was downright terrified. He would never have known the photons were still with him had he not gone in a dark room for one last check. Fear was keeping him from feeling much influence of anything lovely—except for the butterflies that were flitting around in his large intestines.

"Hello. I'm Frederick Nutsell, and this is my science project. My partner is William Bilks, who helped me on it. This black box is a . . . box . . . that I stuck my head into."

"Is that a turtleneck hanging in that hole?" one of the reporters asked. She was a young woman with a big, loud voice, and she was wearing jeans and a rather worn sweatshirt. She seemed to smirk as she pointed to the box.

Nutty nodded and swallowed. His mouth was dry as styrofoam. "Yes, it is," he said.

"What's that for?"

"So no light gets in or out."

"And what's the lamp for?"

"To send light in."

This got a laugh from the crowd, but William slipped Nutty a quick elbow and Nutty continued. "Light has these little things called photons in it. They're very small . . . things. Smaller even than atoms. And they think for themselves sometimes."

"They what?"

A lot of people were crowded around—kids, parents, reporters. Mrs. Smiley was there, and so was Dr. Dunlop, both looking more concerned than happy about all this. And the two scientists had shown up. Most people were grinning now, especially the students, who had shown up with the usual erosion displays or plaster planets.

William, sounding unusually nervous, suddenly jumped in. "No one has claimed that photons think exactly, not in the sense that we do. But they possess a sense for acting as part of a group, a harmony, even when they travel alone."

"What's the deal about him glowing in the dark?" the young woman asked.

"Yes. That's the whole point. Let Nutty explain the rest."

"Nutty? You call the kid Nutty?"

"Frederick, actually. It's just a nickname." But the reporter was writing it down.

"Anyway," Nutty said, "we used these magnets to line up . . . the atoms in my brain."

"The hydrogen atoms," William added. "It's a recognized technique used in a new sort of X-ray method."

"And then William had me really concentrate, which I did, and I guess I kind of went to sleep." This got another pretty good laugh. Nutty was getting more nervous all the time. "And then he sent the photons in, by turning on the light, except it was too hot the first time. I thought my head was going to fry."

This really knocked them out.

"It's not as dumb as it sounds. I'm just not telling it right. See, we were trying to get the photons to start talking with the atoms in my head, and I guess they did, because now I glow in the dark."

The young woman almost lost it, and everyone else was laughing too. Nutty's parents were moving back, little by little, and staring at the floor. Nutty wanted to drift off into photon land, but right now he couldn't get the feeling.

"Listen, everyone. Nutty didn't make that sound as scientific as he might have. But I can assure you that there is basis for everything we did. If you want some proof that something is happening here, take a look in our box. No light can penetrate it. The photons departed and left a void behind them." William tipped the box on its side and opened the top. TV lights came on, but the darkness held. This did get a bit of a reaction.

The two physicists stepped forward and looked very closely. One of them said, "That's astounding," loud enough for everyone to hear.

"Are you sure this isn't some sort of trick?" the reporter asked. She was sounding serious now.

"No, ma'am. And if you'll all follow us to a nearby room, I can assure you that you will see something that will impress you even more."

Everyone walked out of the gym. Some people were still laughing, but the mood had changed, and many were speculating about what the box could mean. William had Nutty stand at the front of the room, as people crowded in, and then he gave another brief explanation of what he thought had occurred.

"And now," William finally announced, "you will see before you evidence that photons of light have actually surrounded Frederick Nutsell's head. We have moved, ladies and gentlemen, into a new era of scientific thought. We are on the threshold of a new world."

The light went off, a second or so passed, and

then a sigh went up, like the sound a crowd makes as fireworks pop overhead. Nutty stood there, knowing he was a science project come to life, the first step into a bold new world—and feeling like a complete idiot.

14

William was standing in front of the black box again, and cameras were clicking and whirring. He was doing all of the talking, and the questions were serious now. He had started from the beginning, explaining every step of the experiment. The two physicists had examined the box carefully again and had expressed their wonder and excitement about the absence of light. Now reporters were going over the facts, trying to comprehend the significance of the event. And William was loving every minute of it.

Nutty, meanwhile, was off to the side, watching and listening—at least at first. He was standing with his arms folded, and every time he felt himself begin to drift away he pinched his arm, hard. All the same, the glow had seeped in around the corners, and he was feeling the joy of seeing William at his best. He liked the reporters and the students who crowded around. He loved his parents, who were so concerned and supportive. People all meant so well, tried so hard to make sense of things.

"Frederick." It was the same reporter who had been so skeptical earlier. "Could you say what you have learned from this experiment?"

"No."

"You mean you haven't learned anything?"

"Yes, I've learned. But I can't describe it. You wouldn't understand."

"Try me."

One of the physicists, a tall man with graying hair, stepped closer. "Yes, I would be fascinated to have some idea of what is happening inside your mind. I'm Dr. David Ramsey, from the University of Missouri." He reached out and shook Nutty's hand. "If photons of light really have gathered around you in the way William thinks they have, are they having some effect that you recognize? What do you know now that you didn't know before?"

Microphones burst into blossom before Nutty, and the lovely eyes of so many friends reached out. "Nothing. They don't teach. They just are."

"Could you explain that?" the reporter asked, and she had her pencil ready.

"Photons are like notes, but they know what part they play to make music."

Silence had fallen as Nutty spoke so softly. He was changed from what he had been earlier, and people seemed to respond to the kindness in his voice.

William said, "He's drifting now, letting the photons have their influence. I have pulled him back from that many times in the last couple of days. I'm not sure what will happen if he gives way entirely. I'll have to call him back soon. I'm going to try to reverse what has happened—for his own protection—and send the photons back to the box."

"But you can't do that," Dr. Ramsey said. "I want to take him back to the university and see what I can learn from him. We've got to verify this whole thing."

"I know how you feel," William said. "But what if he's never the same again?"

"I see no problem there. He seems fine to me—a very nice young man."

Orlando had worked his way in close to Nutty. "Wait a minute," he said. "Nutty's not nice. You don't know what he's really like."

"Yes," William said, and he looked at the professor. "When he's his usual self, he can be quite annoying at times, and frankly, he's only an average sort of kid."

"You don't have any right to experiment with

him and turn him into some kind of vanilla pudding," Orlando said.

"It's all right, Orlando," Nutty said. "I want to be the way I am now. I love you for caring, but you need not be concerned about me."

"See what I mean? Nutty doesn't go around saying things like that. He's not some kind of sissy. You guys don't have any right to make him into one."

Orlando stepped in front of Nutty and pulled him around so that they were facing each other, and he whispered, "Nutty, come on. You don't want to be a wimp all your life, do you?"

William stepped back in. "Nutty, I think maybe we'd better try to release the photons now. Later, we can try to bring them back, if that's your choice, but I don't want you to make the decision while the photons are acting on you."

"Wait." Dr. Ramsey crowded into the little circle around Nutty. "Let me have him for a day or two. I need to find out everything I can before something changes."

"But Dr. Ramsey, what if we can't bring him back to normal? I don't want to be responsible for something like that."

And now Mr. Nutsell was working his way forward, as was almost everyone else. Nutty felt the mood of the people changing. "Just a minute here. This is my son you're talking about," Dad said.

And Mom was saying, "Let me talk to Freddie for a moment. He's not just a scientific experiment."

"I know, Mrs. Nutsell," William said, but everyone was talking at the same time, and Nutty was beginning to be pushed and shoved by the crowd. Another reporter was asking questions, and some of the students wanted to touch his head to see whether they could feel anything strange about it.

Nutty wanted to be away from all this. He let himself flow with the light, tried to push the voices away. But Dr. Ramsey had pushed his face up close to Nutty's. "Frederick, I want to talk to you and your father. I want you to drive over to Columbia with me for just a day or two. It would be a crime not to discover what we can from your experience."

"You don't care about me," Nutty said, distantly. "You don't care about the photons."

"But I do. We need to understand their function, how they relate to wave actions, why they behave as they do. We could—"

Orlando had never left Nutty's side. "Nutty, listen to me," he said. "If he lets you stay in this trance thing for a couple of days, you'll be lost. You'll never come back. Don't let anybody do that to you."

But at the same time Nutty's dad was saying, "Nutty, come here. I need to talk to you alone for a moment."

"Mr. Nutsell, I need to speak to both of you

about this," Dr. Ramsey said, almost shouting over the noise, as so many people tried to have their say at the same time.

"Wait just a moment," William said, and he pushed to stay close to Nutty, forcing Orlando back. "I need to be in on this. I'm not sure anyone else realizes the full effect all this is having—or at least could have—on Nutty."

"Let's get out of this busy room, and talk this over sensibly," Dr. Ramsey suggested. And then Nutty was flowing through the crowd. Dr. Ramsey was on one side of him, holding his arm, Mom on the other, and Dad was walking in front, working his way through all the reporters and cameras and kids and teachers who had crowded around.

And then—wham! Something hit Nutty from behind. Nutty dropped to his knees and felt a body tumble over the top of him. He came back to the world in a sudden leap, and he was stunned by the noise and confusion. Orlando had just knocked him flat, and now he was up and banging Nutty's head with his knuckles as though he were trying to test a watermelon. "Nutty, Nutty, are you in there?"

"Quit that, birdbrain," Nutty said. "Are you trying to crack my skull open?"

"Yeah. If that's what it takes. Don't let these people turn you into anything. Run for it."

Nutty decided he had to get away. He had to

think for himself. He stepped back, but Dr. Ramsey had grabbed his arm again.

"Let him go," Orlando yelled, but Mr. Nutsell was pulling Orlando away.

Suddenly Nutty panicked. He had to get away from all this. He lunged, and at the same moment Orlando jumped forward too. Nutty felt the pain as their heads crashed together, and he felt everything begin to spin. . . . Then darkness.

When Nutty awoke, he was in a dimly lighted room, and several people were around him. His mother's face was close to his, and she was saying, "Freddie, can you hear me?"

"Yeah," he said, and he heard a sigh of relief from those around him.

He heard a low voice say, "Thank goodness." He recognized that it was Dr. Dunlop.

And yet Nutty was feeling something else—a change. "They're gone," he said. "The photons are gone."

"That's right," William said. "When you went unconscious, they must have decided it was time to leave."

Nutty wasn't sure how he felt, but he said, "I guess that's just as well." His vision was getting clearer now. Mom was stroking his forehead, and his dad, who was next to her, reached out and patted

Nutty on the leg. Nutty realized he was lying on a bed, that he was in the nurse's room. He knew he had to have been knocked out for several minutes.

Nutty looked down and saw William, who was at the foot of the bed. He looked very nervous. "What's the matter?" Nutty asked. "Are you disappointed that they left me?"

"No, no. Not at all. It's just that . . . uh . . ." Nutty saw William look at Dad. "We might as well tell him," he said.

"Tell me what?"

"Can you see Orlando over there?"

Nutty raised himself up and looked across the little room. There was Orlando sitting in a chair, with Dr. Ramsey next to him. Orlando was staring rather blankly in front of him. But then Nutty realized. In the semidarkened room he could make it out: a golden glow around Orlando's head.

15

"What happened?" Nutty asked.

Nutty was actually speaking to Orlando, but Orlando seemed not to hear. William answered. "You knocked heads."

"I know. I remember that."

"I guess the photons leaped to the closest brain waves. I think the fact that he was trying to help you made his mind appealing to them—noble and good and all that. In any case, they chose him instead of going back to the box."

"Criminy, William, now what do we do?"

But Dad said, "Son, don't worry about it right now. You've taken a terrible blow. You probably sustained a concussion. You need to rest."

Dr. Dunlop stepped around from the head of the bed. "That's right, Frederick. I've called an ambulance. We'll have paramedics here any minute. You just take it easy until they get here."

"But look at Orlando. He doesn't even know where he is."

"Actually," William said, "he's probably all right. He was never knocked out. He walked down here. But then we all noticed the glow. Since then, I'm afraid the photons have been having a pretty powerful effect on him. The trouble is, we don't dare scare him or slap him or anything. If he has a concussion, that wouldn't do him any good."

"Orlando," Nutty said, raising his voice, "can you hear me?"

"Is that you, Nutty?" Orlando said, in a tender voice.

"Yes. Are you all right?"

"I'm feeling wonderful . . . wonderful. Oh, my dear Nutty, I'm so glad you're all right. You're the best friend I ever had. I love you with all my heart, and I love all these good people who care so much about me. I never thought I would love Dr. Dunlop, but I do. He's a sweet man, Nutty, once you see him for what he really is."

Dr. Dunlop cleared his throat, glanced at Nutty, and sort of shrugged.

Nutty lay back on the bed. He was worried

now. "William, we've got to do something," he whispered.

"Yeah, I know. It's pretty disgusting."

But the paramedics had come through the door, and the two of them, a man and a young woman, seemed to know exactly what to do. They asked all the right questions, and moved very quickly. The man ran Nutty through a quick series of tests, checking his vision, the dilation of his eyes, his memory. And all the while, Orlando was getting about the same treatment. He was not all that easy to deal with, however. He kept patting the woman on the shoulder and telling her how much he appreciated her concern.

"I'm not too worried about this boy," the man eventually said. "He's in no apparent danger. But he was unconscious for some time, so I think it might be well to take him to the hospital for observation."

The woman was still kneeling in front of Orlando. "There's something very strange going on over here. This one is seriously disoriented, and he has some sort of . . . aura or . . . glow . . . or . . . take a look at this kid."

William had been trying to explain to her about the photons, but she had given most of her attention to Orlando. Now William said, "Excuse me, but he got involved—accidentally—with a scientific experiment. The effects you see have nothing to do with the blow he took on the head."

"We'd better get him to the hospital," the woman said. "I have no idea what's going on."

At that point, William, Dr. Dunlop, Mr. Nutsell, Mrs. Nutsell, and Nutty all tried to explain. They more or less surrounded the two paramedics, and they all talked pretty much at the same time.

Meanwhile Orlando had apparently fallen in love with a rubber tree plant in the corner of the room. He got up, went to it, and began speaking to it softly, caressing its leaves. "You poor thing," he whispered. "You look so yellow. You need iron, and you need more light."

Just then the door opened a crack, and someone peeked in. "Orlando." The door opened a little more. "Orlando, are you all right?" It was Sarah.

Orlando stepped to the door. "Oh, yes, thank you. I'm fine."

"What about Nutty?" Sarah opened the door almost halfway. Several other girls were with her, including Mindy.

"He's okay."

Nutty had noticed what was going on. He sat up a little and waved to Sarah—or to everyone, that is.

"You girls are wonderful to care about us so much," Orlando said. "I love every one of you."

"Oh, no!" Sarah said. "Not Orlando too."

"Don't start any stupid stuff, Orlando," Mindy said.

"It's not stupid, Mindy. It's wonderful. I've never been so happy in my life." Orlando stepped toward her, but the paramedics, who had been glancing over, now called him back. At that moment Orlando made a crucial mistake. "Mindy," he said, "I've been so unkind to you in the past. I want to make it up to you. No matter what I've said before, I want you to know I love you now." He reached out for her. "Give me a big hug and let's be—"

Wham! Mindy hit him right between the eyes.

In the ambulance, on the way to the hospital, Orlando woke up. Mindy hadn't exactly knocked him out—but the floor had. He didn't say "Where am I?" the way the guys in the movies always do. He looked around slowly, and he seemed to get the idea. When he saw Nutty on the other gurney, he stared at him for quite some time, and then he whispered, "I tried to hug Mindy, didn't I?"

"Yeah."

Orlando moaned. "How many people know?"

"Too many."

Orlando moaned longer and louder. "I think I'm going to be sick," he said.

The paramedic told him not to talk anymore.

"Orlando, don't feel so bad. Mindy knocked the photons right out of you. She was closest to you, but they went right on by her. William thinks they got disgusted with all of us and went back to the box."

"That's good. I hate those stupid things."

The boys were only in the hospital overnight, and on Monday they were back in school. They took some teasing, even though Orlando threatened to kill anyone who mentioned so much as Mindy's name to him. But Nutty smiled and took his lumps; he just wasn't his usual feisty self.

After school, Nutty went out back. He wanted to sit in the sun and rest for a few minutes before he walked home. He sat on the edge of the sandbox and looked at the sand.

Nutty had only been out there a minute or two when Orlando found him. "You wanna play some catch or something?" he said.

Nutty took a rather long breath and exhaled, the way he had been doing all day. "Not right now. Sit down for a minute. The sun feels good."

"You're not talking to the sand, are you?"

"No."

Orlando sat down next to Nutty. Both of them leaned forward, with their elbows on their knees, their shoes in the sand. Nutty reached down and picked up a handful of sand and let it sift through his fingers.

"Is anything else wrong, Nutty?"

"I don't know. I guess not."

"I keep thinking how lucky we both are. We could've ended up staying weird forever."

Nutty nodded, but then he asked, "Orlando, when the photons were with you, did everything smell really good?"

"I don't know. I was in that nurse's room. That place kind of stinks."

"It's too bad you didn't go outside. When I was outside, the smell was so strong, it was like being in a candy factory or a bakery or something."

"I didn't notice anything like that."

"You didn't get a chance to sleep with those things either. They made me feel like I was floating right off the bed. The air was all soft and warm, and I could feel it rub up against me—the way a cat does."

"Geez, Nutty, you're starting to talk weird again."

"No, I'm not. I'm just trying to remember how it was. Didn't you sort of like the way you felt?"

"Yeah. But it's embarrassing now."

"Why?" Nutty picked up another handful of sand, and then Orlando did the same. Both boys watched as they let the grains run through their fingers.

"I was talking to a plant. And I really liked it. It was like we were old buddies or something."

"That's not so bad, is it?"

"Come on, Nutty. They put people away for stuff like that."

"I know. But we weren't crazy. We just liked plants and trees and stuff."

"Nutty, you were out here talking to sand. Now that's pretty wacko; you've got to admit that."

Nutty nodded. He couldn't deny that.

"And we both told Mindy that we loved her. No one in his right mind would do that."

"I know, Orlando. I know all that."

"Well, don't forget it."

Nutty let it go. He wasn't about to bring the subject up again. He picked up some more sand.

"So do you want to play some catch or not?"

"I guess not. Not today."

Orlando stood up, but he hesitated. "Nutty, I sort of know what you mean. When it was all happening—you know, when I told you I . . . liked you . . . and everything—it seemed like it was okay."

Nutty dropped the sand he was holding and stood up. He looked Orlando straight in the eye. "I like you too, Orlando. I really do. You're a great friend."

"Yeah, right. Uh . . . well, anyway, I'll see you tomorrow." Orlando almost ran to get away.

Nutty sat back down and looked at the sand. And for some reason, he didn't feel like leaving it yet. He picked up another handful, let it filter down through his fingers, watched the little grains. He kept doing that for the better part of half an hour, and he still couldn't get interested in walking home.

Then he heard the voice he half-expected. "Nutty, I've been looking all over for you." It was William. He came over and sat down. "I saw Orlando. He said you were sort of down. It's exactly what I thought would happen."

"You always know what to expect." Nutty smiled. He was really happy to see William.

"Not always. Those photons threw me a few curves."

"Do you think they're gone forever?"

"I don't know. But I think you're missing them now."

"Sort of, I guess. But I didn't want to be weird either. So either way is kind of crummy." Nutty sat down again, and William sat next to him. "I'll bet you feel pretty lousy too. We didn't get famous or anything."

"We got plenty of attention. I don't care so much about that. I just wish we could have gotten a few more answers."

Nutty nodded. And then a great thought hit him, and he knew it was what he had planned to do the whole time. "Do this, William," he said. He hurried and pulled his shoes and socks off and plunged his feet into the sand. William laughed and did the same. They both wiggled their toes and enjoyed the feel of the grainy smoothness.

Nutty glanced around to make sure no one could hear him, and then he whispered, as though William weren't even there, "Sand grains, can you hear me? Look, you guys, I still like you. But don't tell anyone I said so, okay? Let's get together as often as we can and chat."

William chuckled and said, "Yeah, I'll come over too."

Suddenly Nutty turned to William. "Are we still partners and friends and scientific colleagues, and all that?"

"Sure we are."

"Then I have a great idea. Let's go out in front and give my sycamore friend a hug, and then let's hug all the trees between here and my house."

"Great idea," William said. They gathered up their shoes and socks and set off running in their bare feet. They hugged every tree they came to. And when they saw a bird in a little tree, they whistled at it until it turned and looked at them. And then it started to sing. Nutty put his arm around William's shoulder, and the two of them laughed and laughed. Nutty felt so good he got down on his knees and kissed a few rocks, just for old friendship's sake.

ABOUT THE AUTHOR

Dean Hughes is a native of Ogden, Utah. He received his B.A. in English from Weber State College and his Ph.D. from the University of Washington. After teaching for several years at Central Missouri State University, he returned to his home state to pursue a full-time writing career. He has eighteen children's and young adult novels to his credit.

Mr. Hughes currently lives in Provo, Utah, with his wife, Kathleen Hurst Hughes, and his children, Tom, Amy, and Robert.